HOTHOUSE

ALSO BY CHRIS LYNCH

HOTHOUSE

CHRIS LYNCH

An Imprint of HarperCollinsPublishers

HarperTeen is an imprint of HarperCollins Publishers.

Hothouse
www.harperteen.com

Library of Congress Cataloging-in-Publication Data
Lynch, Chris.
　　Hothouse / Chris Lynch. — 1st ed.
　　　　p.　　cm.
　　Summary: Teens DJ and Russell, life-long friends
and neighbors, had drifted apart but when their fire-
fighter fathers are both killed, they try to help one
another come to terms with the tragedy and its aftermath.
　　ISBN 978-0-06-167379-5
　　[1. Fathers and sons—Fiction.　　2. Death—Fiction.
3. Firefighters—Fiction.　　4. Friendship—Fiction.
5. Heroes—Fiction.]　　I. Title.
PZ7.L979739Hot　　2010　　　　　　　　2010003145
[Fic]—dc22　　　　　　　　　　　　　　　　　CIP
　　　　　　　　　　　　　　　　　　　　　　　AC
Typography by Ray Shappell

10 11 12 13 14　CG/RRDB　10 9 8 7 6 5 4 3 2 1

❖

First Edition

To Elise Howard,
for tirelessly battling my attempts
to muck it all up.

HOTHOUSE

ARE YA WINNIN'?

"Are ya winnin'?"

That's my dad, wanting to know if I'm winning. He always wants to know if I'm winning.

There is no competition. No game, no contest, no prize as much as anybody can tell. It's just what he says, his way. His way of asking. How everything is, if everything is all right. It's his how ya doing, and how's life treating ya, I love you and how ya doing.

"I am, Dad," I say. "I'm winnin'."

And I am.

It is a few minutes past six a.m. and we have just finished breakfast because he got home around five and I was already up waiting for him, the eggs and sausages and the yogurt and berries all lined up and ready to roll because

I knew he was coming because I always know when he's coming and it's time to roll with the breakfast. He texted me when he was leaving the station, like he always does, and I was already ready, like I always am. Like it has been since I was just a kid and before that even. Sub-kid, even. Now I'm post-kid and it's as good as ever. Didn't matter what shift he was on, what hour he was coming home, if it wasn't a school night, we were cooking and eating together when he came through that door.

We are done eating now. And having done, having stuffed up pretty good and patted puffed bellies and cleaned up and gotten the kitchen back to mother-approval-level tidy, this is when we would always stagger toward our beds to fall in and enjoy several of the most satisfying sleep hours you could ever know.

Except sometimes. Except like times like this, when breakfast is through but the old man somehow isn't, work and the long night not being quite enough to push him over into exhaustion. Almost like he's gaining energy instead of running out.

Dad wants to go for a walk, just the two of us, to walk off breakfast, before pretty much everybody else has even had theirs.

"Are ya winnin', Russ?"

"I'm winnin', Dad."

"But are ya really winnin'?"

"I really am, Dad."

He loves trees. We're headed for the trees. The sort of arboretum on the hill about a half mile from the house, part of the aggie college over the river. We always head for the trees.

"We should get a dog," Dad says.

"Should we? Why should we do that?"

"What, you don't like dogs? Who doesn't like dogs? What kind of a person doesn't like dogs? I didn't raise no dog-hating kind of a kid."

He likes to pretend to get outraged at things he knows damn well are not even true.

"I like dogs as much as the next guy," I say.

"Not if the next guy is me, you don't. And if you look, I think you will notice that the next guy, right here next to you, is in fact me."

"Then why don't we have a dog, dog-daddy?"

"That's what I was just asking you about, kid,

before you started giving me all this lip about not wanting a dog."

"I never said anyth—"

"Well, we can't be strolling around the neighborhood like this at the break of dawn, prowling-like. Neighbors'll talk. Think we're out looking for hookers or drugs or something."

"Or, they'll maybe think you are a firefighter, which they all actually know and have known forever."

"Well that's me. I was more thinking about you. I'm covered, but you're a teenager, so naturally they'll be thinking along the hookers-drugs line of thinking. Then I get tarred by association."

He can go on like this for a very long time if you encourage him.

"I see your point there, Dad. I guess a dog's the only solution."

"The only one. Nobody brings a dog along drugs-and-hookers scouting. Yup, a noble dog makes everything okay."

"Well, okay then."

"Well okay," he says, spinning around, "let's go get us a noble shelter dog. We'll call him Sheltie."

I grab his shoulder, direct him back toward the nearby trees of the hill.

"Yeah," I say, "maybe in a few hours after the shelter actually opens. And after you've been to bed for a while."

"Maybe that, then," he says, laughing, putting his big arm over my shoulders and pulling me nicely, painfully tight.

It is not the first time we have discussed the dog thing around daybreak.

"Are ya winnin'?" he asks.

"I'm winnin', Dad."

He's yanked a bit of whiplash into my neck, and I am due a few more hours sleep, but I am most definitely winnin' all the same.

TIME LOVES A HERO

My father didn't have any really close friends who didn't have mustaches. It wasn't a rule, it wasn't by design, it just was.

My father was a firefighter, the kind who have mustaches like 1890s baseball players, and all his good friends were that kind of firefighter too. I never quite figured out what the connection was between the look and the man, but the look meant something.

My father helped people a lot, because he was great at so many things—fixing the car, putting up Sheetrock, wiring a ceiling fan, transplanting a rosebush. He liked helping people, helping people was his thing, his profession at work and his hobby at home. People like being helped, I have noticed, and so my dad had a lot of admirers of one kind or another.

Admirers, as opposed to up-close-and-personals. The

guys at the Hothouse—which is what they called their
fire station—were a pure team. They were a team, my
dad and his comrades with their uniform mustaches.
What these guys had was a whole nother thing, inside
itself, outside everything else.

DJ was my friend before I even knew what to do with him.
I have no pre-DJ memories. I am five months older than
he is but nothing ever happened to me before I became
aware of him right there beside me, and so in a reality
more real than real reality DJ and I came into existence
at the same exact time. He lives directly across the street
from me. His father was a firefighter just like my father,
with a mustache just like my father's. The first time we
drew thick Magic Marker mustaches on ourselves that
I can remember was when we were about three, though
there may well have been incidents even before that one.
I can tell you that we did it quite a few times over the
years, and while our mothers were not that keen about it,
our fathers could not have been prouder.

Here's how deep it went. I am named Russell, after
DJ's father. DJ is named David James, after my father,
though you'd only ever call him DJ.

If you called him anything which, mostly, I haven't for

a couple of years now. It was no big thing. In truth, it wasn't even a little thing, as far as I can recall. We just drifted apart. That's what people say, isn't it, when they don't know what the hell went wrong? We just *drifted apart*, even though I can go right to my bedroom window and if I squint hard enough I can still see right into his front window so really we haven't drifted anywhere.

We chose different high schools. I don't know why we did that. Maybe we got tired of living in each other's pocket all the time. Maybe we got tired of firefighter dads who were best friends and moms who were best friends and friends who were neighbors who were class-mates who were best friends.

Maybe. I don't remember feeling that way, but, maybe. We never talked about it.

If I see DJ, I always say hi, so it isn't like that.

We are still right here.

Except we are not.

But then, just like that, we are, again. In that very unfunny funny way of things, DJ and I have *drifted* back together, on one level that we never would have wished on anybody, not even each other. Nobody wants to drift this way.

* * *

It has been three weeks. I have never eaten so well in my life. Ham used to be my favorite food but I believe if I see another baked ham now I'll throw it right out the window into the street and let the dogs all get it. I had my picture taken with the mayor. Nice man, smelled kind of sour. I didn't smile. The house has been full of people all this time, family, neighbors, politicians, sports guys, policemen, firemen, firemen, firemen, total strangers, all kinds of religious types. They come and visit, "pay respects," drop off food, nod a lot, hug my mother, a lot of them wind up crying. Then they sweep, in bunches, across the street over to DJ's house and do a lot more of it all over again, sometimes passing identical groups of folks coming back the other way like an exchange of war prisoners across a border nobody recognizes.

"Pay respects." That's a phrase I am having to get myself acquainted with.

My dad and the rest of them seemed to be always fighting with the city for a better deal and the city seemed to be always fighting back and one time I remember the firefighters' chant was "Pay *Is* Respect." And this mayor, the one right here with the sour smell like he just climbed out of a pickle barrel to pay his respects to my mother and me is the very guy I watched on the news saying "We cannot *afford* any more respect for this firefighters' union."

"I wanted to be sure to come by," he says, solemn as Sunday, "to tell you how much I respected your husband, and what he did for this city."

Right? And I am watching this man, this mayor, give my mother this big bear hug, and I am thinking, How does this happen? How do we get here? How is it that this big fat phony is draped squeezing all over my mother whose husband protector isn't here to keep it from happening?

Until he turns to me. He extends his big meaty paw, which turns out to be also clammy and further evidence of my pickle-barrel theory, and he forces one of those mayor-shakes, a hard and grippy thing that hurts because it caught me off guard. When he's got me, shaking-shaking, he uses it to yank me close, to give me handshake–hug–backslap–smell-my-neck so that all my senses are woozing at once and I am right on the verge of breaking away aggressively except he's in my ear too, isn't he?

"Your father was one tough sonofabitch, Russell. He was Beast."

And like that, he pushes me away again, still shaking my hand, looking hard at me.

I shake him back, only harder, and I look into him, only softer because I am welling up because of course I am but that doesn't mean all the right things aren't also going on inside of me because they are. I feel like a shit for thinking the mayor a phony but it almost doesn't matter because I almost don't remember feeling that way already.

My father got more pay from this very mayor in the end and everybody seemed to respect him and they are coming from everywhere to pay even more respect now because pay may be respect but there is a lot more to it than that. Respect is respect.

And my father was Beast.

The two funerals DJ and I have been to recently are the two funerals DJ and I have been to. We have seen more firefighters wearing white gloves than most people have seen birds. I cried at DJ's dad's funeral even harder than I cried at my dad's. Because of seeing DJ. Because I was seeing him and feeling him and crying for him because he was *there,* I could see him right *there.* At my dad's funeral I cried less because I couldn't see DJ, because I couldn't see one single thing because I was there only for myself. I couldn't feel anything out there at the end of my reach, not even my old friend who is probably the only person on earth who knew exactly precisely what it was like to be me. I can only guess what DJ's reaction was at my dad's funeral. But I *can* guess.

I cannot stand bagpipes. If I ever encounter bagpipes again, there may be violence. If I crossed the street and played bagpipes under DJ's window, I'm sure he'd throw a chair out the window at me. I know this because I know DJ and I know what we have shared, even if we cannot speak about it.

"So, how you been?" I say when I see him the first time after the funerals are over and the strangle of the bagpipes is still torturing my ear bones.

"I've been . . . probably exactly how you think I've been," he says with a slant smile that seems to take some effort.

He has just stepped out of his front door, headed west toward where the bus collects for his school. I came out mine, headed east to catch my own bus. We're not going to school, which doesn't even start again for over a week, but we are dry-running it because here we are. I crossed the street, which I would not normally do. If he appreciates it, it's hard to tell.

"Lots of ham, huh?" I say.

The other half of his smile shows up, which is great. "Ham and bagpipes. Cripes . . ."

I laugh. I don't find it funny, exactly, because nothing is funny now, not yet. But the laugh is real, at the same time. I want to laugh, I'm glad to laugh. "Cripes, is right."

He thumbs west. "I have to get moving, man . . . so do you, right?"

"Right," I say, helpfully thumbing back the other way.

He sticks out his hand.

I shake his hand.

It might not seem like much, not for two guys who have known each other so long. Certainly not for two guys who know so much about each other now. But it is something. It is a long and strong and warm handshake that feels like a pretty decent something as we head off on our east-west ways.

It's the best we can manage anyway. Maybe now, this is the best we will ever be able to manage. You should always do the best you can manage, my dad would say.

"What do you want to do?" Adrian asks me. We are riding the bus to nowhere, and thinking beyond this very bus ride feels beyond me right now. If this were the school run, Adrian and I would have to change once, take two buses from our neighborhood to our school. That feels

like work at the moment, and today I probably wouldn't
even get there.

"Whatever you want to do."

"Russell, don't start this. Not right now."

According to Adrian, I have a history of doing this but
in reality I am the one who has all of the ideas. But he
is right that we have to do something. We have not been
doing *things* since everything changed, and it is starting
to hurt, the motionlessness of life. Thinking about my
dad, thinking about him whenever it gets quiet, aching
for him when it's bad. Adrian wants to jump-start life
again, and he is right.

"What do you want to do?" I ask.

"Right now, I want to knock you on the head because
it's twice already you're telling me to decide."

Despite how it might look, this is progress. People
have been too gentle with me, for obvious reasons, and a
bit of a head-knock would not be altogether awful. What
friends are for, so they say.

We are on the bus. We are sitting at the back like we
usually do, and there are a few other people sprinkled
here and there, older folks mostly, sad-looking drudge-job
commuters, one lady with a little kid about three years
old sitting on the seat next to her and trying every few

seconds to escape before she grabs him again. The bus driver keeps staring back and I am certain he is staring at Adrian and me in that way that bus drivers have of singling you out from far away, making their eyes look huge at the same time they make them squinty and piercing.

"We could go to the mall," I say kind of lamely, while the driver continues to hypnotize me. I don't even like the mall.

"Russ, you're not even trying. The mall?"

"I think that bus driver thinks we did something," I say. "He's kind of worrying me."

Adrian looks now at the driver eyeing us. "How's he even managing to drive the thing?" he asks. "He's not looking at the road in front of him at all, that's what's worrying. How's he do that?"

Adrian finds things fascinating, mostly, or at least interesting. He can forget sometimes to take a situation personally, just because it's intriguing.

And good for Adrian, because right now things get extremely intriguing. The bus driver leans hard on the brakes, and jerks the bus sharply to the curb, and parks spontaneously. It makes that big shooching sound as he jams on the parking break. Hopping right up out of his seat, he spins and thumps with great purpose down the narrow aisle, past the quiet old folks, past the kid who behaves really well now, right back and up to us, close enough he must be able to hear my heart punching me quadruple time in my chest.

He reaches into his baggy blue pocket and hands me a little more money than I paid to get on his bus.

"Sons of heroes don't ever pay no money to ride on my bus," he says, and his hard eyes are very wet. "Ever." He holds out his hairy meaty hand, like he's asking permission to shake. I give him permission, which is only the right thing to do.

"How 'bout friends of sons of heroes?" Adrian asks with outstretched hand.

The driver turns such a look of puzzled disgust on Adrian, it's a wonder he doesn't put him off the bus. He marches back up front. The rest of the passengers are now looking at us. In a few seconds we are in traffic again, on the road to we don't know where. People continue to look at us while they pretend to be looking at other things.

"People know me?" I say low, my turn to be fascinated.

"I guess they do," Adrian says. "You stopped a whole bus."

Adrian waves—at the little boy who hasn't got a clue, to an elderly lady who probably has. She waves back.

"So," he says, "you're some sort of public figure now."

I get a chill, instantly. I don't know this feeling. I don't know that I don't like it either. I just don't know.

Adrian punches my leg, supportively. It helps, a little tiny bit.

"So, where you want to go?" he asks.

"I don't know," I say, but surer. "Let's just ride and see where we wind up."

He's good, Adrian. "Sounds like a plan. Not. But let's."

I have been a firefighter all my life. In my mind, and with all seriousness, that is how I have seen myself. There was never a moment, from the time I figured out what life was and who my old man was, that I did not want to be, more or less, him.

Even right this minute, with my dad dead, with that job having killed him, with my mother being petrified of this very thought, this is the very thought I have: I am a firefighter. It's not even a choice.

There is a big hole in the world that is the size and shape of my father. I intend to fill that hole.

The official world, though, does not know that I already am a firefighter. They have requirements, rules, qualifications, hoops to jump through and mettle to test.

I appreciate that. A firefighter appreciates that, more than probably anybody on earth. You cannot just let any old gump step in and claim a position of this immense responsibility. You have to be trained for this, you have to be committed to learning every angle and following every guideline and knowing the precise best way to perform in every critical situation and then to perform even better. You have to be shown where above-and-beyond is and then go above and beyond that.

> *"Dad, I can't do that."*
> *"Of course you can do that, Russell."*
> *We are standing at the crest of a wheaty-grassy hillock overlooking acres and acres of retired rolling farmland. It is going to be housing, but right now it is in that overgrown halfway-back-to-nature state that is the type of place we seek out and stare at for hours, me and Dad.*
> *"Look at the sign, ya big dummy. It says right on it, DANGEROUS BUILDING—KEEP OUT."*
> *Building is a funny word for it, though so is its actual name, the Teahouse. It's a miniature yellow stone round-tower castle, twenty-four feet high. It's built like one big can settled on top of*

a fatter can, only with all the castle trimmings: keyhole windows and carved faces and with the added cool of overhanging vines and waving wildflowers growing on the wraparound balcony. There is some tasteful graffiti about a guy called Friendly Jed, and some seriously strong metal strapping pulled all around it like a belt holding the thing together. There are also a few huge carved stones tumbled down along the base. My dad wants me to climb this.

"That sign does not pertain to us, Russell," he says with all the confidence he has, which is all the confidence in the world. "They never meant that for the likes of you and me."

"Is that a fact?" I ask, taking one backward step for every step he takes toward the Teahouse.

"It is a fact. Let me tell you, my kid, that some of my most memorable runs were scored when I ignored the third base coach and ran right through the stop sign. I have told you what a stellar baseball player I was in high school."

"You have, Dad. But you can tell me again if you want to."

He only ever boasts when he is in a certain

kind of uppy mood. I never know when this mood is coming, but it is a mood I always want to prolong. I don't mind at all if it means rehashing hardball glory days. And it sure beats dying in the rubble of the Teahouse.

He waves me off, modesty coming back to him. "Ahh, pfft," he says, marching up to the little castle and its sign for other people. He raises a foot, touches lightly in a seam, a crevice, feels around with the foot the way an elephant does with its trunk, until he finds the spot he wants and he is up off mother earth and living on the surface of the Teahouse.

"I wish you wouldn't do that, Dad," I say.

"And I wish you would," he says.

He is not a small man. He's not light, or lithe, or anything that would make you think he had any business two feet off the ground, never mind twenty. He is a substantial man.

And he is also up the side and to the top of the crumbling stone Teahouse before you can say mountain goat. Not a pebble is dislodged in his ascent.

"Now, you do it, son."

"Do what?" I demand. "Fly? I can't do what you do, Dad."

"Course you can," he says, laughter of real disbelief wafting down toward me. "You my boy."

Damn. I hate it when he says that. Because, of course, I love it when he says that.

I approach the Teahouse with caution, like any sane person would. My dad stands there up top with his hands on his hips and his grin on his face looking very much like the Jolly Green Giant.

"That's the boy," he says. "Test it, find the stability. Feel it."

I do what he says, but partly I am doing what my bones already know. I can feel the stability. I get my toes into crevices that will hold me. I work my fingers into spaces I can pull from. Misstep, misstep, nothing serious, some crumbs fall, tumble along the wall to a crackling landing in the rubble at the base. I feel a big stone wiggle in my hand, then shift substantially, fifteen feet off the ground.

"Russell!" Dad calls, the first note of real concern coming out as a full symphony.

I look straight up into his face looking down,

worry and gravity folding his features into an unmade bed with a mustache. I grin up at him.

"If it's all too much for you, old man, maybe you should just look away until the scary part is over."

He returns my smile now. "You my boy," he says, as I pop up in his face at the top of the tower.

"You are indeed," he says, giving me a two-slap back-pat hug.

We turn, not quite together, looking out over the roll of the landscape. Dad's scanning in the direction where the small regional airport has grown to take up about one-third of the old farm-land. I look off the other way, to where the hill farm is still almost obvious but obviously fading.

"It's not bad," Dad says about the airport. Local opinion is well divided on that. "I think it looks good, as part of the landscape. Almost hand-some, even. I'm going to fly out of there someday. Did I tell you that, Russ? My plan to learn to fly? After I retire, I think. Or maybe I'll start while I'm still in the service, since I have all those open days and all. Have I told you that, how I plan to fly, after I retire maybe a little early?"

*"You have, Dad," I say, looking over where he is
looking now. "But I don't mind if you tell me again."*

I can't believe how nervous I am. When I finally get back,
to Monday-night YFF training, I could just about puke
with the nerves I'm feeling all up and down my torso.
What a baby, huh? I have been doing this for so long, two
whole years, and knowing these same people and really
completely at home with it all and, what a baby.

Three hours, every Monday night. Medic training,
mouth-to-mouth, putting out real fires that we start ourselves, learning how they start and how they finish, what
a firefighter can do and cannot. I was already a teammate,
with these other youth firefighters, a family. I have blown
my breath into everybody in the room, for godsake, and
every one of them has done the same to me.

And now I am so nervous, butterfly nervous, I can
barely walk through the door to pick up my training, for
my life, which had been knocked sideways only a few
weeks before. Sideways and legless, much like I feel now.

It takes several minutes of standing like a dope, listening to friendly familiar voices through the door, but
finally I turn the knob and push on in.

To something like an ovation.

It doesn't start big. It starts the opposite, in fact. All conversation stops as everybody slowly turns in my direction, a lot like the scenes of the wake and the funeral when I walked in, scenes we all know I never wanted to relive and would surely de-live if I could. I shocked them, even though I think they all knew I was coming back. Now they've shocked me and we've shocked each other into a kind of paralysis and awkward smiling until The Girl takes over.

I don't mean anything by it, calling her The Girl, because that is what we all call her, this tall, slim, square-shouldered only-girl who started training a couple of weeks after me. Week one, there was prejudice, I have to admit. By week two, I knew. I saw it in her, that part of her that was just like me, and the reason she so belonged here. By week three you were just ignorant or hateful if you didn't see it, and whichever it was, you didn't belong here. That was when she became The Girl permanently to everyone in the squad including The Girl herself. I nearly forget now, but I think her name once was Melanie.

The Girl starts clapping, after our squadwide awkward silence. First very gently and slowly, but then more sure, then joined by two and three and ten and two supervisors.

I am becoming the world's foremost authority on the skill of not crying when you feel like crying. Sad things make me want to cry, like watching out my kitchen window one morning and seeing a jackass cat pick off a contented nibbling bird at our feeder. Happy things make me want to cry, like hitting my tenth consecutive free throw at the corner playground for the first time in my life. I never made it past eight before, usually because Dad would start woofing at me and making me furious and distracted. He never saw me hit the ten, and when I did hit the ten I never saw the flood coming because I wasn't counting, wasn't playing that, but just knew when I hit it what had happened and what wasn't right about it.

I miss my dad.

And proud things make me want to cry. Like a roomful of people who know better paying tribute to some combination of me and the old man, blending us into one immortal hero of a timeless firefighter.

Hard as it is to fight the tears, is it weird to say I don't mind this at all?

"Get back to work, ya damn babies," I say then. They need to get back to work. I need to get back to work. I go across the room, to where The Girl is standing with a dummy at her feet. I don't mean me. Sitting on the floor in front of her is the victim, a hundred-pound floppy doll we use when simulating rescues. He wears a size small priest outfit somebody put on him long before I showed up, and he goes by the name of Monsignor O'Saveme.

"Need some assistance with this one, ma'am?" I ask The Girl in my simulated-hero voice.

"Not at all," she says with a smile. "But you may borrow him if you are so inclined."

I take the victim and heave him over my shoulder. I walk him to the corner, where an unnecessarily tight spiral staircase leads up to the second floor. Up we go, for the first steps of the next phase of my firefighting life.

Jesus, the monsignor is heavy. Most people I know weigh more than one hundred pounds, but Lord, this victim always manages to make himself heavier and more awkward than one hundred pounds would ever figure to be. He does it on purpose, I always figured, because he is part of the team. This is his job, and everybody on this team does his job to the max and so he is maximum heavy and maximum awkward.

And now, somehow he is even worse.

"You been putting on weight while I was away, ya fat bastard?" I say as I get halfway up the spiral.

"Maybe you're weaker," he says.

I drop him. With a fat, thwacking, hundred-pound thud, I drop him right there and down the stairs.

He is very real. His head, his back, his legs, bapping off the stairs, rolling, smacking, bapping again, all of it so sickeningly real in sound and look and feel, I have my hands clapped to my mouth through the whole ordeal until Monsignor O'Saveme finally mercifully collapses there in a heap at the bottom of the stairs.

It is a horror movie. I stand there on the stairs, still holding my face, while everybody looks at me, at the victim, at me again. Like I am some old movie queen about to swoop down the stairs for my big entrance, only without a head or something.

"Ah," I say, "sorry, but that had to happen. The monsignor just let slip that he's a Yankees fan."

Nervous laughter of relief fills that awful sucking void of silence as I descend the stairs and everybody makes busy again. "Suppose I have to save him anyway, huh?"

I am kind of shaking, though, as I bend down to scoop him back up. "Care to repeat that?" I say, tough but not brave. I have him tight by the dog collar in case he doesn't get the message. No response. "Didn't think so," I say.

And so I rescue him, quickly up the stairs and then back down again, the fat father causing me to sweat like there is a real fire lapping around me.

I don't believe in ghosts. Of any kind. And I don't believe I am any weaker. Even if I have been thinking it, it's not the same as believing it and it's none of the monsignor's damn business anyway.

I am not weaker. And I will be stronger. Than ever.

"You all right?" The Girl asks when I return her victim to her feet where I found him.

"Of course I'm all right," I say.

"Little out of practice, though," she says with a shrug.

"Suppose," I say.

"And a little out of shape."

"Okay, I get it."

"It's to be expected," she says, both giggling wickedly and touching my arm warmly. I get a little buzzy, from the arm part.

"There's a party," I say without giving myself any warning. "A summer's-over thing. You like beach parties?"

Her name *was* Melanie, it *is* Melanie. We meet at the seawall, at the concrete ramp that leads down directly from the fried dough place to the beach proper.

"You want some fried dough?" I ask.

"You want some barf?" she answers.

If she were any more a natural-born firefighter she'd have a better mustache than mine. I am glad she doesn't.

It is a mostly flat ocean as we walk the half mile of white to the party. We head about halfway down, to where the tide-flattened sand is pavement-walkable but still smells of sand. It is on its way back in, the tide, and this bit will be water again in another hour. The evening is just-so gray, no hint of sun but no hint of rain, so cool enough. Adrian's family has been hosting this end-of-summer splash for the last few years, and this being our senior summer there was no way this show wasn't going to go on no matter what.

"You okay?" Melanie asks, and we know what she is referring to. The *what* of no matter what.

"I'm okay," I say. "Maybe not life-of-the-party okay, but certainly okay enough to be a part of a party."

"I'm glad," she says.

"I'm glad you're glad," I say.

It is a modest little beach house but that's all it ever really needed to be. Adrian's folks' real house is only a few miles inland and they only ever bought this one because somebody died in it. It involved a leaky gas stove and an old bachelor and his dogs and my father told me about what a god-awful rot the place had become by the time the rescue services showed up. So it was kind of a steal, and the stench of death was less of an issue if all you really needed was to use the shower and the fridge and the private patio on fine days with the windows open and host a lot of kids who smelled like death much of the time anyway.

My dad was everywhere in this town. He touched everything. There is no escaping his reach so it's a good thing I'd never want to.

"You've never been here?" I ask her as we start up the beach, away from the quiet ocean and toward the unquiet house.

"No," she says. "Been by it, of course, but that's all."

Melanie doesn't go to the same high school with Adrian and me, so our circles aren't entirely the same. She goes to the same school as DJ.

It isn't a huge party—maybe twenty-five or thirty people—but it fills the house and patio pretty good. Adrian is standing where the seawall butts right up to the property when Melanie and I approach. He has his foot up on the wall, and is looking out into the distance like an old sea captain on the bow of his ship.

"Permission to come aboard, sir?" I say from the bottom of the weathered wooden steps.

He looks down at us. "Permission for the pretty one, aye," he says.

I start up the stairs. Melanie grabs the back pockets of my jeans and pulls me down off the third step and into the sand. "He did not mean you," she says.

"You are really strong," I tell her.

"Do remember that," she says.

"Strong, and pretty, aye," Adrian adds.

"Aye," Melanie agrees.

Physical strength, beauty and self-confidence. Why did I bring her here again?

By the time I make my way up the shivering weather-worn steps, I am already alone. Captain Adrian has piped Melanie aboard his ship and I just mount the wall in time to see him leading her into a crowd, into the house.

I don't mind. My favorite part of this house was always the seawall anyway. As soon as I am over it, I sit back down on it and watch.

The first floor is basically a kitchen back on the road side, with a small bathroom attached, then a decent-sized caramel-paneled living room and then a screened-in porch facing the beach. Another porch is plunked on top

of that one, with separate doors leading into two bedrooms. From where I sit it is like a display party, porches
full, windows and doors open and likewise peopled by
the people I know who are all about to be seniors.

And somewhere too that old guy who died in there,
and his dogs, who stunk the joint up. Not that I believe in
ghosts, but it is probably only fair to imagine them there
too. Party on, ghosts.

I am enjoying myself, doing nothing, small sea breeze
at my back and a weird distant social mash-up playing
out in front of me but not quite with me. I am enjoying
myself enough to not really notice the brown bottle of
beer doing its little *drink me* dance in the air in front of
my face.

I take the beer.

"DJ?" I say, surprised, and not unhappy, to see my oldest old friend. Like I said, this is not his school crowd.

He sits down next to me. "My dad said he vomited
for like twenty minutes straight when they found the old
man and his dogs in there. Said it smelled like burning
hair and rancid pork boiled in vinegar."

"I remember. That's exactly what my dad smelled like
when he came home. He took a bath for four hours. Every
time the water cooled off he just refilled the tub."

DJ nods. "Canned goods and a kettle."

That's what they found, basically, of the old guy's life. Of his kitchen life, anyway. That's what he lived on, until he didn't. That's what my dad kept saying and, apparently, DJ's dad too.

"Canned goods and a kettle," I repeat.

The sea, I can hear, is creeping up closer behind us. The tide is coming in and the flat little waves are making their broad crispy noises by raking back through the line of shells and pebbles not far off. DJ aims his beer bottle at mine without looking at me. We clink as we watch the party.

"Russ and Dave. They are everywhere, aren't they?" he says, then sips.

"Everywhere," I say. "Long may it last."

I expected something. A repeat. Maybe not the words, exactly, but the feeling. I get a muffled grunt instead.

So I help. "Amazing. How two guys could cover so much ground, so much life, the way they did around here. I didn't think it was possible, but I actually think I'm getting prouder as—"

"You going out with Melanie, now?" he asks me, bluntly.

"No," I answer, bluntly. "Just asked her if she wanted

to come along. She's in Young Firefighters with me. What brought you here, anyway? I didn't expect to see you."

"An invitation brought me."

"You know Adrian?"

"Not really. But enough. You know how it plays, Russell. We are invited everydamnplace now. We are America's guests, me and you. Standing invites, anywhere, anytime, anywho. We are stars, brother."

We clink glass necks again, in the most uncelebratory way possible.

"Sounds like you don't like it, DJ. If you don't like it, why don't you just stay home?"

DJ drains his beer, stands up, looks out at the coming sea and then at me. "Because I want to be home even less, Russell."

It's sad and a little wobbly, his voice, and his expression matches. Then it's all gone again. "Beer?" he asks.

I look at my bottle, half full. "Beer," I say.

Before DJ has a chance to return with my next beer, before I even have a chance to kill my previous beer, I am surrounded. It's like the first day back at school, with everybody congregating in the school yard to compare long hot summers. Even though I haven't been away, in any real, physical sense.

"Dude," Cameron says.

My people don't really say *dude* to each other. That's the first sign. That things are not quite in the correct cosmic order. It is even, apparently, an organized approach, my old friends creeping up with caution once I am obviously alone. Didn't want to approach, really. Didn't want me alone though, either. Jeez, not that. I have seen them all at points, mostly funeral points and wake points and other such unnatural occurrences, but this, you would have to say, is the first real, live connection we would attempt to make since. Funny, guys seem to forget how to talk to a guy who has suddenly, spectacularly misplaced his father.

"Dude," I say in response to Cameron and the weirdness.

Cameron gets it. I can see him visibly relax, exhale like the sea, let his shoulders fall back to their natural slump. The stupidity of a well-placed *dude* can really defuse a situation. He shakes my hand. "You doing all right, Russ?"

"He's still dead, if that's what you mean."

It just came out. I think what I meant was to make light, to break ice, to help us all through the awkward moment that then would leave all the awkward moments behind us so we could enjoy something like a party and something like life from this point on.

That was what I meant. What I get are two other things entirely. First, all the eyes in the lowering light go white as Wiffle balls. Philby and Jane and Lexa and Cameron and Burgess, folks I've known and schooled with and joked with for years, all go dead with bafflement over what I said.

Second, though, is even worse. Second is what I did to myself. I choked myself, was what I did. The words were meant to show that I could handle it now but the fact is that I can't, not quite, not now, and it takes every bit of my control not to spoil it all even worse by letting my face tell the truth.

Firefighters come to the rescue. As they do.

"A toast to heroes," Melanie says, wedging herself in tight next to me on the wall. DJ, sitting in tight on her other side, hands across a beer.

Everybody toasts heroes.

"Toasted heroes," DJ quips.

"Wow," Adrian says, leaning in and clinking everybody in reach, "you guys are hard-core."

"Gallows humor," DJ says. "It's the very bedrock of the firefighter community. Think nothing of it."

"Anyway," I say, "toasting yourself there too, Melanie. *All* firefighters are heroes."

"Until proven otherwise," DJ adds cheerily, initiating another round of clinks.

Despite our best efforts, the crowd is beginning to relax and talk with something like the old familiar freeness. Adrian backs away into hosting; somewhere inside music creeps up a little louder to compete with rising tide and breeze.

"But you really are," Melanie whispers, very close, breathy on my ear. "Both of you, heroes."

She hangs, just there, for a few seconds, breathing after talking, and who could argue?

"Thank you," I say.

She slaps my leg and goes back inside. That leaves me staring at DJ, across the empty space that was Melanie. With a grin, he slaps my leg just like she did. Except a lot harder than she did.

"Having fun?" I ask into his broad curious grin.

"Nope," he says, slapping my thigh again.

"Is my leg somehow responsible?"

"Sorry." His *sorry* is real, though he slaps me again.

"Try and have fun, DJ," I say. As with so many times in the past, I bounce my own time off of what I read on his face, and his face is reading uncomfortable now. I want him to start getting over it as much for me as for himself.

"I am trying," he says, waggling the beer bottle in front of my face.

Philby interrupts with a snack bowl, which he shoves between us. The combination of Doritos and shrimps in the same bowl confirms the absence of any parental input here.

"What a great idea," DJ says, mashing up a fistful and working it into his mouth.

"You guys know each other?" I ask.

They shake hands while DJ chews.

People are starting to pair up, I notice, both here at the party and for the longer haul. Philby and Jane have been circling each other for a while and it was fairly assumed that they would go through the events of senior year hand in hand. Same pretty much for Lexa and Burgess. This is all coming together and is all right by pretty much everyone.

Was I dramatic to think, for a minute, that the events of my life would have somehow derailed these things? That anybody's life out there was not going to go on as planned?

"So you are not going out with Melanie?" DJ asks.

"I said I wasn't," I say, again.

"Well you wouldn't be the first guy to say something like that and not mean it."

"I mean it." I turn to face him. "This would be a curious point in life for me to start lying to you, now wouldn't it?"

His hard smile then loses just that bit of the crystal-cut edging. "Of course it would," he says, patting me lightly on the cheek.

"You are unusually handsy tonight, pal," I say, gently taking his hand and placing it in his own lap.

"I am, aren't I?" he says. "I should probably have a beer."

"Are we drinking all their beer, though?" I ask. "Did you bring anything? I didn't even bring anything."

Adrian, passing by, reaches over and gives the cheek another mild slap.

"Don't you dare," he says, jolly, deadly serious. "You hear me? You just drop that shit right now. If you two *ever* have to buy another beer in this town I want to hear about it because somebody's going to be due an ass whippin'."

Without pause, Adrian is on his way again.

"Kinda cool, huh?" I say, standing up now next to my oldest and dearest. "I mean, how nice does that feel?" I pat his shoulder.

I feel his shoulder muscle tight as a baseball in my hand. "Let's go drain every goddamn drop," he says fiercely.

We don't drain every goddamn drop, but we make a solid effort. It is a nice party, a warm and breezy finish to what has been an unbreezy summer, and a decent approach shot at the better eventful year to come. The music is kept at a mellow level, glasses never break, fights never develop, bedrooms are not violated. Maybe it is the somber element DJ and I brought, maybe it is the newly mature and responsible air about us turning seniors and experiencing real life more than we had intended, but the party is a more dignified affair than last year's or the year before. Some people, I suppose, might be a bit disappointed by that. I wouldn't know. If they are, it doesn't show.

We are all, in fact, pitching in cleaning up as Adrian prepares to close up shop not too long after midnight, in accordance with the pretty fair and reasonable no-parents arrangement. There is even Simon and Garfunkel music coolly soundtracking the housekeeping as if to have the parental types there in spirit.

"Canned goods and a kettle," I say at the same time S&G say hello to darkness their old friend. I am washing up a sampling of the perfectly beach-house collection of mismatched drinking glasses in the old tub of a beige enamel sink. I shift on my feet, feeling the puckery sheet linoleum on the floor where the old man was found somewhere right here near me. Where the old man was found by my old man, right here near me. I imagine it clearly now, the scene. Not the grisly, not the befoulment, the decomposition and the dogs and that. I picture the remnants of the life that my dad came into when he came into this place. I see him seeing the canned goods and kettle, and wishing more than anything he had gotten there in time to sit down to a cup of tea with the gent. For every "stench of death" detail he ever brought home from this gig, he brought home thirty-five hundred little swatches of quilts and slippers and whiffs of baklava and bitter home-perm hair junk that made up the lives and deaths he crashed through with some regularity.

And I think, That was the hero stuff. I know, that was the hero stuff.

"Nice work," Adrian says, his chin on my left shoulder as I dry a tall textured avocado-green glass. "You are the kind of guest who is always a joy. Thanks for coming."

"Thanks for having me. And now, you are brooming everyone out, correct?"

"Largely correct," he says.

We turn from the sink, head out of the empty kitchen toward the living room, Adrian snapping off the light behind us. The majority of people are gone, a handful of stragglers, straggling, waiting for me, apparently, which I particularly appreciate.

"Where is DJ?" I ask. Normally, I would not have asked. I am not my brother's keeper, as I am barely my own, but there was an unsettling feeling about him to me, this evening, and I just want to see him all right.

"He's all right," Adrian says, snapping off that light as well and shepherding us out through the screened porch. "He said he would rather not go home. Asked if he could borrow the house."

I double-take, then figure why not. Home will be there tomorrow.

"Is that within the rules?"

"Not technically. But I'm not saying no to him, and you know, neither are my parents."

As we stand on the patio now, DJ's voice floats down over us.

"Another fringe benefit," he says.

We turn to look up at him, and Melanie, leaning over the porch railing, with beers. "Thanks, Dad," he says, holding up his beer in the direction of the wide ocean.

It's getting hard to distinguish between surf sounds and people gasping.

"Keep a low profile," Adrian advises the couple as he leaves them with his house.

"How low should I go?" DJ asks, his beaming grin and outstretched beer making him a pervy little Statue of Liberty.

"Just get in the house," Adrian snaps, and Melanie pulls the lad inside.

As a bunch of friends walk up the beach, the high tide now snappling in one ear, I'm thinking that *getting the girl* is generally considered to be the high-water mark of a young man's evening. There are, though, even finer, and rarer happenings, and one of them is when you recognize a moment when you have a breathtakingly great friend. When Adrian bumps up close and speaks to me over the crunch of tiny defenseless seashells, I have exactly one of those moments.

"That's kind of shit, man," he says. "Now you got no father *and* no date."

You have to be a breathtakingly great friend to say something like that.

I continue looking straight ahead, the baby white-caps flickering at my left peripheral, the luminous white sand doing similar off to the right. The girls, Jane and Lexa, let out gasp-squeals of horror and the guys, Burgess, Philby, and Cameron, make uh-oh noises down deep in their throats. Adrian, though, knows just how to proceed.

Nudge. He prods me at the back of my shoulder. Then again, a little harder, then again until I lurch forward, and burst out laughing.

"She was not my date, jackass," I say.

He bear-hugs me from behind and lets me drag him along the sand as everybody exhales, laughs, and contributes to the discussion of what a slime Adrian is.

"I'm sure you will do better tomorrow, Russ," Cameron adds, "when girls see your imprints in the sand."

I look at my feet as I walk, seeing Adrian's feet together dragging a deep trough between my footprints.

"Fine," I say. "I'll take all the help I can get. With you all marrying up at a worrying rate, I'm going to wind up having to take my mother to the prom."

"Too late," Adrian says. "Your mom already asked me to take her. Don't wait up."

It is perhaps possible to have too good a friend. I drop Adrian facedown in the sand.

"You could go with Cameron," Adrian says into the sand. "Nobody's buying what he's selling, either."

Cameron silently walks on top of Adrian's prone body, including his fat head.

"Well done," I say.

"Thanks," he says. "Doesn't mean I'm not interested, though."

"I'll get back to you," I say.

It goes on like this while it lasts, and in its quiet uneventful way this is the finest time I've had since my dad died. Quiet and uneventful were underrated in my head before. Friends, even, were underrated. They all seem like more now.

We lose Jane and Philby at the foot of the lifeguard stand. Burgess and Lexa make it as far as the ramp by the fried dough place where Melanie and I first hit the beach preparty and all. They are suddenly quite tired and need a short sandy rest.

Lexa kisses me on the cheek. "You're a brave guy," she says, mistylike like girls can get by the water, late at night, so I've heard.

"For what?" I ask. "For living?"

She kisses me again, this time right near my mouth, which feels right and wrong and wonderful. "Maybe for that, yeah," she says, backing away toward her man.

"Okay," I say, a grateful smile stretching my face. "I'll take it."

Cameron is now standing right in front of me.

"What?" I ask.

"Have you decided yet?"

"Ah, no, Cam, I'm still working on it."

"Okay," he says, "then I'm going to walk the beach some more, as long as we're still free agents."

"Good luck," I say, and Adrian blurts, "Safe sex . . . or the other kind," as Cameron heads across the sands.

Adrian and I walk on in the direction of the neighborhood proper, which is two or three miles interior. All the small beachy businesses are closed as we pass through that unrealness into the substance of grub town life.

"I like that," he says, maybe ten minutes beyond the beach.

"You like what?"

"I like what you said to Lexa, 'Okay, I'll take it.' It's a good attitude, in light of all."

"Hey," I say, shrugging, "I'll take anything. I'm not proud."

He gives me a backhand knuckle slap in the ribs.

"Like hell you're not," he says firmly.

I laugh. It can be nice to be caught out. It can be joy to be known.

"Like hell I'm not, true," I say. "Adrian, I gotta tell you, I know it's not mine, exactly, I know I haven't

earned anything, but I am so insanely proud, of everything remotely connected to my father. I want to scream
with it, I'm so goddamn proud, of *myself* somehow. Am I
mental? Am I shitty?"

He grabs my shirt at the shoulder, walking along at the
same time, shaking me all over while he talks. "No, no,
no, no, hell, no Russell. Jesus, I hope you don't smack me
for this, but I feel the same, exact way. Just knowing you,
knowing your dad, just touching it like, that much . . .
Jesus, I'm getting goose damn bumps and choking up
over it just trying to tell you."

He lets go of my shirt, holds out his arm in the warm
late air, and I can easily make out a full range of tiny flesh
mountains.

"And I can promise you," he adds, "that everybody
feels the same. Even if most of 'em probably can't say it to
you, they're feeling it."

I hold out my arm, to compare my own childish, awkward bumpiness.

"I'm glad you can say it, anyway," I say.

"I can. You're a hero, just go ahead and take it, take
it all."

I walk on a bit like that, holding out my arm and looking at it. "Okay," I say. "I will."

* * *

Lots of the time, it's more like a great friend has up and moved away on me. Without telling me he was going. Without calling or writing after he left.

I wake up at night pretty often. I always woke up at night pretty often but that made sense because I would get up to meet my dad and we would eat.

Firefighter's shifts are weird things anyway, but my dad put some effort into making them even weirder. His shifts would be twenty-four hours some days, ten hours other days, fourteen hours over nights. Then he'd be home for four days straight. But what I loved was when he would come in at the odd hours—six in the morning or twelve at night. He was always volunteering to do extra this and that at the station because, he said, "I got the next four days off to rest up." But really, because he loved that fire station, and he loved those guys. "Hunker in the Bunker" was what he called hanging out at the station. "Firefighting is a team sport," he told me over and over. We both looked forward to the day when I would join the team and we could fight together.

Not that he didn't love coming home to us, too, because he did. We had the best of times when he would come home, and the best of those best times were when he came home at those odd hours. Because then it felt like there was nobody else on the whole ball of earth but me and the old man.

And we would cook and eat together. Just like him and his pals at the station. Always, it was breakfast when he came home. Scrambled eggs and fried tomatoes and bagels and sausages and pancakes from a special batter that he taught me only after I promised never to reveal it to anyone who was not a member of the firefighters' fraternity. My mother steamed when I wouldn't tell, even though her pancakes are nearly as good.

And here's something that happened. I developed a sense of when he was coming home. I knew when his shift would end, but that wasn't hugely helpful since he could come home one or two or five hours after that. But whenever he was finally on his way, I would pop up, right out of my bed like somebody was cranking the crank and I was jacking out of the box. For real. I was always up just when he got there.

He loved that, I think. You should have seen his moods when he would come home and I would be there waiting. Usually I'd have all the gear for breakfast all lined up and ready to roll. Should have seen how he loved it.

But now, sometimes, I wake up like he's coming, and I completely forget that he isn't. Like this morning, at five thirty, I am standing at the stove scrambling eggs and I don't even remember getting here. I am staring at the eggs as they start to burn just a bit, and the burning shakes me, the smell and the crust developing on my usually perfect scramble.

When I finally fully realize what I am doing, what a stupid thing I am doing . . . I continue doing it.

I leave the gas on high, and I stand there, staring at the eggs as they crust up, as they curl and harden and blacken, as the smoke goes thick and comes up to me and I breathe it in as deep as I can, and I'm choking and blinded with it.

"Russell!" my mother says, rushing into the kitchen and bumping me away from the stove. I reel, stagger back, coughing and hacking and rubbing madly at my eyes. She takes the disaster of a frying pan and shoves it out the back door onto the porch.

"Oh, Russ," she says, rushing back to me, "are you all right?"

"I burnt the eggs, Ma," I say to her.

"So I smelled," she says, inching closer with her arms wide.

I don't let her get at me, holding out a stiff arm like I am a running back trying to evade tackling. With the other hand I rub busily at my smoke-wicked eyes. I am so stuck right now, so hopelessly stuck between I don't want to be babied and Christ I am such a baby.

"Can I not even cook eggs now without him?" I ask. "I thought I was doing all right. I thought . . ."

"You're doing all right, Russell. You are doing much more all right than anybody could ask."

I am embarrassed. Needing this, I am embarrassed. My mother doesn't need this. She needs a man around here and I am supposed to be that man.

"I'm sorry, Ma. Go to bed. I'm just being dramatic. Jesus. I'll clean up. I'll take care of everything. Just, go on now."

She stands at her short distance, the smoke smell filling the air between us along with everything else. She doesn't say another thing, doesn't try to touch me again.

But thank Christ she doesn't leave either.

Ma goes to the refrigerator and takes out the carton of grapefruit juice, collects two glasses on her way, and sits at the table with them.

It takes us about a silent half hour to get through that carton of juice. She's good company, and helps me a lot just by being there, and she of course knows that.

But it isn't anything at all like sitting down to very

early or very late breakfast with my dad, and she of course knows that as well. Dad's mood across this particular table was something so sky-high in the morning, I sometimes found myself wondering how to re-create it during the normal daytime hours when he would sometimes go all quiet and unexplained dark at mealtimes. I tried, a couple of times, to surprise him with breakfast in the middle of the daytime, hoping to make our special thing happen, but it never quite worked. I guess that's what makes special times special, the fact that you can't just whip them up.

"It's at night mostly," I say.

She reaches across the table and puts her hand around my hand around the empty juice glass.

"I am mostly okay in the daytime now," I tell her. "Mostly."

"I know. I do. Nights, I'm afraid, may be tough for a while yet, Russ. But I'll be here, so I'll hold you up, and you hold me up, and maybe we'll agree that neither of us will burn the house down in the meantime. It's a modest plan, but a good place to start, huh?"

It's a very good thing she didn't go to bed when I told her to.

I nod. "Now, lady, you can go to bed. I'll clean that pan."

"You, your father, and God together couldn't clean that pan," she says, getting up and patting my head on her way by. "But good luck."

I'm in the gym. We have a deal, a sponsorship really, with the local Ramada. The Young Firefighters have free membership. It's not state-of-the art, but it's got enough, though the pool takes about a hundred and fifty laps to make a mile. You get dizzy before you get winded.

I have just finished working out for a solid two hours. I would still be going if I could. My head likes the workout at least as much as my body does, but there is a limit. So now I'm steaming. I go back and forth among the steam and sauna and whirlpool after a good workout, and the well-cooked-pasta sensation I get, barely able to crawl out of the building by the end, well lately it suits me just fine. It's almost peaceful.

I always think straight thoughts in the sauna especially. The sauna seems to do to my head what a hot iron does to a wrinkled shirt.

High school diploma or GED, minimum. Must be at least eighteen years of age. Volunteer work helpful. Firefighting and EMS training highly desirable but not required. Military service preferable but not necessary.

A life. A firefighting life, you would think they would mention. I have a lot of qualifications to gain and a lot of time to get there, but I am already part of the service in profound ways that cannot be measured. They should know this, and should be able to factor it into my case. But I am no kid, certainly in this world at this stage, I am no kid. I realize they have to have their requirements and I have to put in the time and effort to reach those requirements because they cannot have just any old scrubs signing on to the service. You have got to be special. You have got to be special, and I have got to be patient.

But I am growing the mustache. It might sound stupid, but it feels important. I am building the body and the mind as hard as they can be, and I am growing the mustache. Nobody is going to confuse me for an 1890s baseball player yet, but getting started on this is my quiet, for-myself way of feeling that little bit closer to the service, to the guys, to the team. That much closer to the man.

I am staring at my shadowy reflection in the smoky glass door, opposite my high bench seat in the sauna. I can almost see the man.

"Somebody's getting ripped," The Girl says, slipping in through that same door.

"Hi," I say.

She climbs up to the top bench next to me, sits right close. She is wearing an electric blue bathing suit, Olympic swimmer type. Her figure is Olympic swimmer type. I was not previously aware.

"You been doing triple sessions at this place, or what?" she says, lightly squeezing my biceps.

We are the only two people here, but it's still extremely embarrassing.

"A little more than usual, maybe," I say, and politely pull from her grip.

"'Roids? I'm betting 'roids."

I feel far too weak for this. I start to stand.

"Jeez, it's getting awfully hot in here," I say, and lean to leave.

She grabs the seat of my shorts and pulls me back down with alarming ease. I am weak.

"Don't be antisocial," she says.

I lean back against the scalding wooden slats of the bench. Remarkable, how if you move off them after getting accustomed to them, they instantly become foreign and searing again. It's not the worst feeling.

"So, you enjoyed the party," I say.

"I did. Thank you very much for inviting me. What a great group all around."

I suppose I do expect her to go somewhere with that. She doesn't. We sit and become one with the heat. It's almost like a sound, it's so baking. The Girl leans back alongside me, feels the same hot slats across her back.

She makes the sizzle sound, "Tssssz . . ." but she doesn't flinch.

I am no good at this. "So, DJ . . ." I say.

"DJ," she says.

We sit and listen to the heat some more. That's it.

I stand for real now, and The Girl is happy enough to let me. "I'm completely noodled," I say, stepping down to more breathable air. I see my ghosty reflection again as I approach the door.

"Look out for him," she says as my hand rests on the door handle. I turn. "Just keep an eye. He's not as strong as you are, I don't think."

I shake my head, and head out of the heat. "Don't be fooled. I'm not as strong as I am either."

Firefighters insist on doing stuff. Everything they do seems to require bigger motion, more action than the regular one-foot-in-front-of-the-other routine of most people's days. And since these days are anything but routine, they are now insisting on doing something big.

They are being honored, DJ's dad and mine. By the Hothouse, at the Hothouse, with a big public show-off of a permanent memorial.

There is to be a big department-sponsored t'do for the two Outrageous Courageous heroes of the community. *T'do* is my mother's term for any organized gathering we are required to attend, especially if she would really prefer not to attend.

"Sheesh," she says after getting off the phone. "This is one t'do I could really do without." She plunks herself onto the couch. I plunk beside her.

"Well you can't just t'do without it, Ma," I say.

"I know that, Russ. I understand there are a lot of situations where you have to do things you don't want to do, because people feel they are doing those things for you."

"Well they are doing it for us."

"Yes. Yes, of course they are. And because people do something nice for you, you do something nice, for them, by attending. Everybody thinks they are doing the nice thing for somebody else, while all parties would probably rather stay home and watch TV, but in the end something nice has probably been achieved even if it might be hard to identify what that was."

It's a different sound coming out of my mother now. Weary. Burnt.

"It will be great," I say, slowly rising from the couch. "I know there has been a lot of *stuff* we have had to do, but this one feels different. This one's going to be about the good stuff. I don't think people would rather be at home watching TV than doing this, and I know I wouldn't. I'm going to let myself get a little excited about this one."

She smiles. "Okay. I'm just glad I don't have to go."

"Like hell you don't have to go."

"Of course I'm going to go," she says, still weary, but a little less weary. "I wouldn't want to miss your happy, beaming little proud face."

"Okay, lady, if you need to mock me to feel better, that's fine with me." It's a price I'm willing to pay.

She slowly tips over sideways on the couch, tucks her legs up, and settles way deep in. Sweet and innocent is how she looks as her smile turns vertical on me.

"I wasn't mocking. I do see your happy, beaming little proud face. And it is making me want to go now."

I make a point of beaming just a bit more as her eyes close and I leave her, surely with the both of us thinking about the fine Outrageous Courageous t'do to come. *Outrageous Courageous* was also not my phrase. It is common speech now, in the newspapers, shouted at us from cars, even spray-painted huge on a wall of the fire station, erased, and painted right back again. It is the shorthand for my dad and DJ's, used as often as people speak their names. I love to hear my dad's actual name, and don't want it ever to fade away.

But I *love* Outrageous Courageous.

"How come you're not a better bowler, Dad?"

"I am a better bowler."

He gets in moods like this, where he doesn't make any kind of sense at all. It tends to be a funny nonsense, but I can never tell where it comes from or where it goes to again, so the erratic part I don't care for. Sometimes it makes me a little angry.

"Better than what?" I ask, deliberately interfering with his release.

His fourteen-pound ball squibs off right and just barely clips one pin before toddling off into the gutter.

"Better than that," he says, staring for a long time at the lane and the confident pins and what went wrong.

"If you're better than that," I insist, "then bowl better than that."

His ball rolls back up the feeder. He collects it and turns to me.

"Are you angry with me?" he asks, holding his ball up high like a big fat second head.

"I just want you to be better," I snap, gesturing for him to address the lane instead of me.

I see sad disappointment flicker across his face, then he turns toward the pins again and I feel like crap.

"I'm sorry," I call out, again just in time to wobble his release, only this time unintentionally.

He knocks down three more.

I have no idea. I have no idea why I need him to be better at this. I have no idea why his weird slanted smile at knocking down only four pins in a frame of tenpin bothers me so much.

"Relax," he says, taking the seat next to me at the scoring desk. "That's why they call it bowling."

I have no idea what that is supposed to mean. I have no idea why it makes me so angry to hear it that I want to just walk right out and leave him there.

But I don't. I do the better thing, and I bowl. I knock down eight pins with my next ball and my dad is clapping enthusiastically for me. I know he means it, but I don't even look around at him.

"What is wrong with you?" I snap, waiting for my ball to return.

"There is nothing wrong with me," he says, the cheeriness of only a few seconds ago vanished. Killed, actually, by me.

My ball returns and I use it to pound down the last two pins. He doesn't clap. We don't talk. The mood remains grim for the rest of the game, and the inappropriateness of it bothers me every bit as much as the inexplicable cheer that came before.

Adrian and I have finally gotten back to something like our regular bowling rotation. We normally go at least once a week and often twice but with the things that have happened, bowling slid down the list of priorities, even though with the things that have happened bowling would have been as welcome an event as any I could think of. One of the beautiful things about the nature of bowling is that when I am at it, I can almost leave all the rest of the stuff behind. And that happens to be one of the beautiful things about Adrian's company, too—that he can make me feel like I am somebody other than that guy who lost his father. So the combination of Adrian and bowling is like some great sensory deprivation tank in my life, only with scorekeeping.

Unless something unusual gets in the way.

First, we go to pay for our two strings and our joker shoes, and the guy behind the counter, a guy I have seen hundreds of times over the years, with his timeless ageless sad acned face, just shakes his head grimly and backs away from the counter. He looks almost spooked, treating the money like it's a live grenade or some voodoo thing that will haunt him forever if he touches it.

"Thank you," I say, but he just shakes his head again and waves me off like I shouldn't even be doing that much.

"I could get used to that," Adrian says.

"You probably shouldn't," I say.

We walk up to lane eight, toting the goofy shoes. "Check it out," says Adrian, pointing.

It is a poster, and it is posted here in our private getaway from everything. It's on red paper with black lettering and looks like a seven-year-old did it with a marker and made photocopies. It's taped to the ball polisher, with several others distributed around the place:

OUTRAGEOUS COURAGEOUS BARBECUE
MEMORIAL DEDICATION
SATURDAY NOON TILL AFTERNOON
MUSIC BY THE LEGENDARY
HOTHOUSE HEROES
BRING EVERYONE, COME OUT AND PAY
TRIBUTE TO TWO OF OUR OWN

"What's with firefighters and barbecuing all the time?" Adrian asks. "Whenever they get together they're firing it up. You would think hot coals and flammable liquids would be the last things they'd want to see on the day off."

"*One of ours*," I say out loud, staring at the cheap poster.

"Nice of you to share," Adrian says.

"Well . . . you're welcome," I say. "And really, I'm happy to share, and I love the fact that everybody wants to share my dad. . . ."

"Right," he says, "it's like, a community thing. Like they are part of this community and this community is proud—"

"And that's really great. But I have to say, seeing it here, right here"—I tap the words on the poster—"I just get this little jolt, this shock of, selfishness is maybe what it is, but part of me thinks, well the *community's* dads didn't have their faces burnt off, did they?" The way I fire-breathe the word *community*, I could be aiming to burn unfortunate Adrian's face off. "The *community* goes home at night and eats supper with dad, and dad is there and so is his face. So the 'our own' thing . . . it's great, but it's . . . no, it's great."

I don't like to be reminded about their faces but this is how it is. Lord do I not like to be reminded about their faces. Details. I can't swerve the details when I think about it and I always think first about slow motion, the heat, the force, the flame, the smoke, curling back over my dad's face, over Russ's face and the first thing I see—because my rotten mind never lets me not see it—is the way the heat melts, curls then melts, those two magnificent thick mustaches, and that starts it and then like pulling a shade back from that lip up over . . . his face, all his face, his cheeks, Russ's eyes . . . my father's eyes, drying . . .

"People are just trying to be nice, Russell," Adrian says calmly so that I don't scream. "They're just trying to be in there with you. And don't get angry at me but, you know, I'm proud of your dad too. I can't help it, I'm just like everybody else. That's a good thing, I think."

The part of me that has been playing the scene of my dad's melting face, the scene nobody else has to live with, wants to scream right in Adrian's face and remind him that he gets to share this great community pride with his own *father* who works, who's alive, cozy at home two days every week so they have lots of time to chat about stuff.

Good thing the better part of me gets the better of that part of me.

"That is a good thing," I say. I nod a bunch of times. "It is a good thing, Adrian." I brush past him on the way to the lane, bumping into him a little on purpose.

It is, it is a good thing. It's just a good thing with bad moments.

When I think of Mrs. Kotsopolis, that's one of the bad moments. She has lived in this neighborhood since the beginning of time but will not be at the Outrageous Courageous barbecue to commemorate the heroes of the tragic fire. Because Mrs. Kotsopolis was in the tragic fire. Right now she is very much in the hospital.

I knew that Mrs. Kotsopolis used to be a teacher, because she came to my school, something like fourth grade, to talk about how it was, that long ago, being a teacher. Sounded like a great time to be a teacher. Less of a great time to be a kid. She left us old-time teacher gear to keep on display, as a reminder, so somebody would remember, she said. She left us a big brass bell with a wooden handle she used to call the kids inside with. I don't remember any of the other stuff, but the bell really looked like something from another world. Memorable, you know? For sure she would have had a number of other old teacher-life mementos around her house to remind her own self of the days, and for sure those details would have gripped at my dad something fierce. I know I know and I know we would have been talking about the old handwriting chart, or classroom flagpole or ancient leather-bound class register book or pull-down map of an unrecognizable world, for days, after he got home from saving Mrs. Kotsopolis and her house and her life from that fire.

Details kill me. If I could erase the small details of everything, like chalk wiped from a blackboard, I might do better with that smudginess. It might go smoother.

I also remember that cat of hers. Hasn't been seen since the fire. It was a smoky gray, almost blue, and it followed her to my school and sat on the outside windowsill the whole time she spoke to us. Old Mr. Kotsopolis had died not too long before and I feel sorry now for thinking then that the lady and the cat seemed to need something to do with themselves. I thought they didn't appear to know what to do with themselves when actually they were doing it. I do feel sorry now. I feel really, really sorry.

He's a very old cat now. I hope he found someplace.

Everybody from the Hothouse is here. Everybody who knows anybody from the Hothouse is here. And everybody those people know is also here.

The Hothouse is what the guys stationed at my father's fire station call the place. It's something said with great pride, something that when you hear it, it makes you say, Jeez, I wish I was part of that, part of that Hothouse thing.

And today, everybody is. I mean, *everybody*.

The fair-size paved lot surrounding the Hothouse on three sides resembles a fairground but with better people and better smells. The charcoal and beef and pork is thick in the air, as are balloons in bunches tied up and bouncing against a streaky whitey-blue sky. I can see a stage set up around the back, and the huge half-barrel barbecue puffing smoke, and quite a few dogs stiffing and straining toward the food but generally behaving themselves like creatures who do not want to be banished. Local radio is playing geezer-rock out of big speakers and if every person who lived within a two-mile radius of the Hothouse came out today this is exactly what the crowd would look like so I'm guessing that's pretty much what we've got.

"I'm outta here," I say as we approach the throng.

The crowd is overwhelming, but I'm just being dramatic.

"You're not going anywhere," Adrian says, putting a friendly aggressive arm around my shoulders.

My mother has drifted about twenty feet ahead of us, as Adrian and I have been walking progressively slower the closer we got to the sounds. He starts tugging me along a little faster. There is a murmur, then a rustle, then almost a commotion, as our arrival gets noticed and the crowd turns on.

"Wow," Adrian says, "you guys are stars."

Even Adrian's firm helpfulness isn't firm enough to move me now. I stop short. As I stand like a dummy on the sidewalk, I watch my mother stride purposefully in, into the embrace of a loving crowd and the beginnings of actual applause. She's come around pretty well to the idea, I'd say. As she gets folded into the love and adulation, she encounters DJ's mother, and they hug each other warmly, and long. DJ stands there, looking immensely uncomfortable.

Even from my distance, applause feels nice, awkward nice. Even though it is applause that doesn't technically belong to me, it feels like it is for me and it's an amazing sensation because how many times do you get applauded in your life? I think in most lives, the answer is none. Or pretty close to it.

"Go on," Adrian says, giving me a little shove, "give the people what they want."

I put my nose to the air. "It does smell good," I say.

As soon as we hit the grounds, Adrian peels away and I am totally swamped by people who I assume mean me no harm but look very much like the horde that tracked down poor Frankenstein's monster. Only they are waving burgers and Cokes instead of flaming torches. I know they mean well, but it feels like a lot when you are surrounded, and it's hot, and everybody is talking and a lot of them you've never even seen and they are pressing close like they are your best friends.

My old best friend is pressed in exactly the same sandwich. DJ is a few feet away, dealing with a dozen people at once just like I am, looking as sweaty and confused as I feel. He inches a bit in my direction, manages to extend a high flat palm, and I manage to slap it.

I feel just that little bit of a bit less anxious.

Jim Clerk makes it all better. Jim Clerk is the

commander of the Hothouse, and the master of ceremonies for the t'do. He is six foot three, with brilliant white hair and white teeth and a speckled gray mustache. He looks like Teddy Roosevelt's kinder older brother and has a voice like fog blowing through an oboe and he was my dad's boss.

"Okay, folks," says Jim the fog. "Okay, folks, a little space here, spread things out just a little bit now."

Kind Jim Clerk, which he pronounces *Clark* for some reason but his reasons must be good ones if he states them in that voice, has experience calming crowds and taming unruly situations. In seconds he's got one big paw on my shoulder and another on DJ's shoulder, and he is leading us through a clear path where hyperventilation is no longer necessary. In what must be against his every impulse, he is leading two scared guys toward the smoke.

And if I tell you it is glorious smoke, I am coming nowhere near to doing the scent justice.

You could fit me and DJ onto the grill entirely and still have room for, maybe, a whole pig. There are burgers and giant sausages dripping fat onto the coals, and hot dogs and quarter pieces of chicken, potatoes in foil, corn on cobs, buns. Off to the side is a great vat of barbecue baked beans with fat chunks of pork suspended like tiny bobbing heads of flabby seals. There is a table with brownies and homemade flapjacks and nearby is a retirement-ready firefighter named Danny Mullins with a serious frown, churning his own fresh ice cream. The first time Danny handed me one of his homemades— mint chocolate chip—he had to give me a second one ten seconds later. The third one my dad had to hold for me while I licked because my hands were not up to the job. They were only three-year-old hands, after all. I am sure I recall Danny smiling more broadly every time I messed it up that day.

This day he looks a hundred and seventy years old, and smiling seems to be not in the cards.

"Is it all a bit much for you men?" Jim Clerk asks DJ and me. Then he answers reassuringly, "It is all a bit much, isn't it. Yes, it is. Well you just stick by me as long as you feel uneasy and I'll take care of you. Starting with, I'm going to feed you. Everything is better and manageable when you are being fed. Am I not right about that?"

It does help, I think. My dad was almost always eating, or cooking, or preparing, or plotting, foodstuffs. He wasn't fat—though he wasn't thin, either—but his relationship with food was a passionate one, and he was famous for it.

"You're not *not* right about it," I say.

Jim Clerk laughs his laugh like warm honey. "As your father would have said," he says. "And he just may have cleared this whole grill on his own, if he was of a mind to."

I am still not sure what this feeling is I feel, when people who knew my dad say things about when he was here. I am proud and sad and I want to applaud and cry at the same time and I want to tell them to please stop and I am afraid that they will stop. But the one thing I am certain of is that I demand when somebody says something about my father, my Outrageous Courageous, Hothouse Hero of a dad, that particular something had better be true.

"This is true," I say, and enjoy saying.

I inch up to the grill and start pointing at things, like a hungry animal with fingers but no power of speech.

DJ, I notice, is likewise speechless, but he is holding back, looking off away, squirmy.

"Your father was a great man," Jim Clerk tells DJ as I offer him a cheeseburger and take a bite of my own.

"I know, thanks," he says. He takes the burger but shows no sign of an intention to eat it.

Martin Rowe walks up to us. A stocky, smiley guy, Martin is also in the band. He has a mustache. "I'm boycotting the food today," Martin says, patting his belly with both hands, indicating that this does not happen often. "Because if Russell's thirteen-alarm chili couldn't be here, my stomach is taking the day off out of respect." He gestures toward a big empty stewpot propped on a chair. Tied around the pot is the apron DJ's dad wore when it was his turn to cook at the Hothouse. In bright flamy red letters, it says, *Russell's Cooking—You've Been Warned.*

DJ smiles a fractured smile at Martin and nods a thank-you. He pulls the burger up near his face, moves his lips a bit. But it's more like he's holding a stuffed animal rather than something to eat.

The food is every bit first-rate. The local dj on the booming radio is making everything sound like a real party, and calls out to us personally so many times I'm starting to feel like he's here, doing the play-by-play. He's not, but he has certainly been filled in.

I keep hearing my father's name, and DJ's father's name. On the radio, very loud. In my ear, in my face, so very loud. One woman says she came from an hour away and her brother is a firefighter wherever she lives but he couldn't come because he is on duty protecting everybody just exactly the way my father would have done. She is sweet and kind and talking a little too close to my face and she holds an adorable three-legged puppy up to me, it's a little Jack Russell and she tells me how he lost his leg in some fire-related way that I simply cannot understand but I do understand when she tells me the dog's new name is Dave Russell after her two heroes.

DJ does an about-face at this, keeping his back to the woman while he looks everywhere else.

She gets all weepy and kisses me on the cheek before backing away with all red and dripping eyes and I wonder how she is going to drive all that way back home like this. She may need firefighters yet, today, is the joke I tell myself to try and hold it together.

"Hang in there, pal," says another firefighter I have known since before I knew. His name is John DeVellis, and though he has no mustache his face plays like it does so it's okay. If John were not a firefighter he could be employed as a fireplug, such is his build. Five six, barrel chest, shaded specs, brilliant white teeth always shown off with a smile, and salty-pepper hair that splays out in rays exactly like how I used to draw the sun over this firehouse in school as a little kid. I might have been drawing John all along.

"I'm hanging, pal," I say to John.

He hands me a plate with strawberry-rhubarb pie, warmed and melting its ice-cream helmet. He puts his helmet on me, too. Much as I love John, I wish he wouldn't. I'm not a kid anymore. I'm really not. I can't be.

I cannot find my mother. I wonder if she's all right at the same time as knowing that she is. Part of me feels like wondering and worrying about her is supposed to be my thing now.

DJ is better because truly food does make you better if you let it, and because DJ is a strong person in spite of Melanie's warning. Stronger than me, I always thought, and I have no reason to stop thinking that now.

We talk to a lot, a lot of people, which is to say we mostly listen to a lot of people come up and tell us how unbelievably great our dads were, and our mothers are, and we ourselves will be over time. It's very much like a dream, where the people are people you know, but at the same time they're not.

"You'll be great," says a woman who is crying, quietly but steadily enough that rivulets of tear water are carving canyons down her face. She is my parents' generation, and I know I should know her. I know I do know her. It would be a good time for my mother to be handy. "You come from greatness. And you'll be great."

"Thank you," I say in a way I hope is familiar enough. "I'm going to try."

We say thank you a lot, me and DJ. Then it is time.

"It's time!" booms a voice even louder than the radio guy's voice, cutting him right off as we go live and everybody migrates toward the big stage and the beginning of the big show, the highlight centerpiece of the whole day. The performance of the Hothouse Heroes, with the unveiling of the tributes.

"Folks, what can I say?" Jim Clerk says when the mad cheering has calmed a bit and he certainly knows what he can say. "Russell and Dave were the best of us. They were"—and here he chokes, not for the last time—"the best we can do. They dedicated every bit of themselves to the job, to the ideal, that we all strive for. To do whatever it takes, to be the fire wall between all harm and the people of our community who we hold so precious. . . ." He trails off under the thunder of love and crowd madness that rolls right up over us from the back of the crowd, and over our heads. Fifty different hands slap my back, and I feel DJ beside me being bounced forward and forward with the same thing. I notice for the first time, as Jim dabs at his eyes and wipes his flushed face like he's battling a real fire right now, the buckets. Along the front lip of the stage, a row of old-timey tin fire-brigade buckets stands guard. Rather, they stand for collection.

People are walking up, like some kind of revival meeting, and howling things as they stuff money into those buckets. Dollars, coins. Some drop gently, some jam. Some sharpshooters even throw from a few rows back, but it is accumulating rapidly.

We're even getting paid for this.

I look at DJ, and he looks down at the ground.

"And what these two kings did, giving their lives, is what every single one of us, each and every member of this service would gladly do. But the difference, my friends, the difference is, they *did* it. And there isn't a person in this crowd who is surprised that Dave and Russell were the two men who gave their lives that day because they *were* Outrageous Courageous . . ."

The crowd goes beyond mental here, in a way that makes me every bit as proud as I am frightened of the power of it.

". . . and they *were* the Hothouse Heroes, *our* heroes, *your* heroes, and we are here to testify and to celebrate today . . ."

I cannot hear what he is saying anymore. DJ has his hands covering his ears. I see my mother walking onto the stage, arm in arm with DJ's mother.

It feels almost like we are being physically crushed

from behind by the crowd even though, in reality, they are more like protecting and cocooning us. Then, holding us. Then, lifting us.

Oh God, they want us onstage. They are motioning DJ and me up onto the stage, as the band, the Hothouse Heroes minus two, settle into position with their instruments.

"No," DJ says, though I am the only person in this world who can actually hear him. "No, thank you anyway, but I'm good right here." His actions—as much as you could call them actions—don't really back up his words. He falls into the crowd's embrace like he is a stuffed DJ effigy.

It must give him some comfort that I am on the same crowd-surf to the stage, and we are never separated for a second. We remain so close, in fact, that I am able to crane my neck a little, and take a good healthy bite right out of that burger. I smile with accomplishment as I chew, and if I have helped loosen him up at all, his wince is nevertheless not a celebration of comfort. He shoves the burger at me, like you do when somebody has polluted your food so you don't want it anymore.

"Quite a t'do, after all, isn't it?" my mother shouts into my ear as I am delivered and the crowd somehow manages a higher gear of delirium.

"It's a t'do and a half," I shout as I lean back into her and weakly wave out at the fans. Beside me, DJ's mother has her arm tightly around her son's shoulders. DJ is peering one by one into the brigade buckets of money, which are still filling up.

"We might never have to work, our whole lives," he says joylessly into my ear.

"I'll work anyway, just to be near the common folks," I say truthlessly into his.

"Now you all know," big Jim says, reclaiming control of the proceedings, "what dedicated and gifted musicians have always wound up at this very firehouse. . . ."

Behind him, the individual band members start cracking up.

"Don't be modest, men. And, it's no secret that Russ and Dave were as talented as anyone in the industry . . . Russell on the banjo and Dave on mean fiddle. . . ."

There. There is where it can't go. As I said, I can listen to a lot of uncomfortably wonderful things being said about my father, can even listen to a superhuman barrage of them to make a guy's knees go weak like today. But the rule's the rule—it's got to be true.

I turn right around to catch Jim Clerk's eye. He looks down at me.

"What?" he asks, bagged.

"Come on," I say.

He's stifling a laugh now. "He was a great fiddler."

There are a fair few murmurs, in the band and out beyond, but nobody's going to step into this one but me.

"He was awful," I say.

My mother gives me a playful shake of the shoulders, and parts of the crowd boo me in defense of my old man. And I get a shiver like I haven't had since. Since, the night I shivered myself to sleep.

It is the best Dad moment I have had, since I haven't had the dad.

It's got it all. It's real, and it's fun. It's got loyal and it's got great and it's got true.

Just like the man.

This is so hard. Beautiful, but so mind-splitting hard.

"He was not awful," Jim plays along.

I nod defiantly, because words aren't coming now. He had only played the thing for a year and a half; he was self-taught. He had no musical anything in him but he learned just so he could be in this band right here, because he wanted to belong to everything, anything that was happening here, with these guys.

But really, when he practiced, cats came to the house in gangs to free their tortured comrade.

"He did not stink," Jim finally says. "Dave was . . . earnest, on the fiddle."

The crowd roars approval, and finally, DJ jumps in. "But my dad was a *great banjo player!*" And this statement seems to please him more than anything else so far.

He was great, too. Russell was great at whatever he did. Russell was a star.

The band starts a slow, gentle plucked rhythm, swampy, pale-blue bluegrass and Jim shouts out, "Friends, the Hothouse Heroes!" and backs away, pulling back a curtain at the rear of the stage.

Sitting together on adjacent chairs, necks crossed like old friends, my dad's fiddle and Russ's banjo.

Hanging up on the wall behind them, is the memorial.

It is big, five feet by five feet, mixed-media. There are two oversized brass replicas of the city FD badges, but with the names *Russ* and *Dave* engraved. The badges lean on each other at an angle, like the comedy/drama faces at a playhouse. An eagle spreads its wings behind the badges, and in front of him a ribbonlike banner flutters above and below carrying the words *OUTRAGEOUS* and *COURAGEOUS.*

Hundreds of people gasp at once, but they all sound like my mother to me. I turn back and look at her. She has her hand covering her mouth, and her eyes are blinking three times the speed of the three-beat pattern as the band plays "Waltzing Matilda" right at us.

"You all right?" I ask her as she squeezes my shoulder hard enough to get juice out of it.

"It's all right to cry," is what she says.

"Go ahead," I say, being, you know, the man round here now.

"I meant you," she says.

"Me? I'm not crying."

"If you say so," she says with a smile and another mighty squeeze. There's the juice again. "If you're not, you're the only one."

I turn back to the stage and watch the goings-on from head-bow angle now. See, don't be seen.

Beside me, DJ's got the same idea, different approach. He has plunked right down to the ground, sitting cross-legged, staring up, and out, at nothing in particular. He is moving just slightly with the music, though, so something okay is going on, too. I give him a little wave, like we are in sight but far apart. He gives me a small nod. Just.

The band—four floating mustaches behind guitar, accordion, drums and upright bass—plays on for an hour of Cajun, country toe-tap, hillbilly ballroom niceness that

makes the people sway, and sing, and even swing some.
Even the upbeat numbers are tearjerkers, but it all still
manages to be more or less encouraging, even when God
noses his way in with the spirituals near the end. Their
big finish is when they get almost hopping on a bluesish
dad-rock thing called "Time Loves a Hero." Going by
the title, and the band's relative mastery of the song, I'm
guessing it is their signature tune.

Time loves a hero
but only time will tell . . .

Signature or not, the song is the perfect storm that
sends the gathering into a kind of madness, brutal sing-
alonging, passionate shouting of more mostly true testa-
ments to my dad and DJ's, and an emptying of pockets
into those tin buckets.

Exhaustion.

"Everyone loves your dads."

The man who says that to us, as DJ and I sit on those
empty chairs in the middle of the empty stage at the
head of the emptying grounds, is pushing a gigantic
broom. The broom is just about the width of an average
car, and I think if the guy could just attach it to one he

could clean up this mess in about two days. He doesn't seem to mind, though.

He is a firefighter. All that's left is us and firefighters. You could tell, even if you didn't know them, which of the people here today were in the service because they all made a point to wear something from the gear. Famous fire helmets, many of them. The big black boots and suspenders. The badge. One guy even marched around all afternoon shirtless, but with his badge somehow secured to an inhumanly hairy chest. Velcro is possibly the answer there. This firefighter here, though, never seemed like he loved my dad, and my dad felt much the same. His face and eyes are now the same strawberry color with crying, though.

"Thank you," DJ says wearily to the guy. He plucks at my father's fiddle strings. Now my fiddle strings.

"Ya," I add, "we kind of got that impression." I plink at the banjo.

I'm gladdened a little by the way he mentioned our dads in the present. That they are still loved right here now by other people as well as us.

Gladdened is not the word to use for DJ.

"They don't know anything about it, do they?" he asks the only person who probably exactly does. "They say all these things and remember so much, and put up empty chairs for show. . . ."

"You're hurting that," I say carefully as I ease the fiddle out of DJ's harsh fingers. I give him the banjo. "They don't know. They can't know, exactly—"

"No, they can't," he snaps, "so they should probably stop *commemorating* and *sharing* now, and get on with their own little lives."

I feel myself physically pulling back from the force of him.

"I'm sorry, guys."

As soon as I hear the kind velvet voice behind us I want to slither right inside the curly carved holes in the fiddle's body. I can't manage it so I panic and scrape the bow all over the strings instead.

"Come on now," Jim Clerk says, "your father played better than *that*."

I am thrilled to hear the joke at this moment. "I am sorry, Mr. Clerk—"

DJ is on his feet. He's hopped up and lurched in Jim's direction like to babble apologies and hug and beg. . . .

But actually, he doesn't do anything.

"We tried our best," Jim says. "We didn't mean to upset anybody or to intrude. Maybe it was too much. But please understand, what you saw today was love. It was real. And believe it or not, all those people here today needed this. People need their heroes, DJ. They need their legends and their greats. And that was your dads."

DJ does not look like he is about to say something this time. But he doesn't look like he's going to burst into flames, either. Which is encouraging.

"But we're done now," Jim says, and suddenly his big smooth smiling face pulls in on itself like closing curtains. He reaches out and plucks awkwardly at the strings of Russell's banjo. "And so now, you take this, you take it all, you take your feelings for your dads and your memories, take them home and keep them nice. Do that for yourselves, okay?"

He doesn't get an answer. He does, but it's not loud. DJ clutches that banjo and I clutch this fiddle and we stare at big Jim and Jim stares back. He puts that great smile back on, and it is still a great thing but it is great and beautiful the way a three-legged dog is even though it's not what it could be, not what it's supposed to be, not what it was before.

UNDER THE BRIDGE

"Are ya winnin'?"

"Jeez, Dad," I say, springing up in the bed so fast that our foreheads clunk like coconuts and I fall right back again.

He laughs, rubbing his head. He laughs.

I squint at my clock in the darkness. It is neither late enough nor early enough to be seeing him.

"Is it breakfast time? How did I not wake up if you were coming home? How did I not know—"

"Shush," he says, reaching out and patting me on the chest. His big paw is radiating heat. "Shush, shush. You're all right. I'm home early. Boss sent me home early. You want a baklava?"

"No. Why did he send you home? Are you all right?"

"Oh, I'm fine. It's just this knee of mine. You know how I hurt it. It's fine. It's just acting up a

little, swelling up a little. Big Jim thought I should take it home to rest. That's all."

That's a relief to me. Relief that I have not lost my sense of when Dad's shift is ending and breakfast time is coming. And in the firefighter game, a gimpy knee is a pretty benign thing to get you sent home.

"Oh," I say. "That's good. But . . . he sent you home with a bad knee? You worked a whole four-day shift one time with a broken wrist before going to the hospital. Why would he send you home for this? And why would you go?"

He's still got his hand on my chest. Reminds me of the hot water bottle my folks would always put on me for colds. It is heating up, like a fever, as he speaks.

"Guess I'm getting too old to act like that anymore. Guess the boss knows when I should be home. Nothing to worry about, though."

"Oh," I say, though I had stopped worrying there until he told me not to.

"The important thing," he says, "is, are ya winnin', son?"

"I am, Dad. I'm winnin'. Are you winnin'?"

He takes a long time to answer. The heat off his hand increases more in the time.

"I am, son," he says. "Of course I'm winnin'. Listen, you go to sleep now. I shouldn't have gotten you up."

"It's okay," I say. "I only have the crap classes in the morning. I can catch up then."

"Ah," he says, laughing. He pushes down on my chest, sinking me back into the mattress and back in the direction of sleepland.

He closes my bedroom door very gently, like trying not to wake the baby.

A minute further into sleep, I believe I hear him go back out into the night.

Old Mr. Kotsopolis had run a Greek coffee shop in the neighborhood forever. He ran it in the days when his wife was teaching and ringing that brass bell, and he ran it for years after she retired. Sometimes she would be behind the counter, but mostly he ran it on his own. My dad told me the primary business of the place was all the older Greek guys playing cards for money at the back, but he personally spent so much of his own cash gathering up dewy fresh baklava and powerful coffee for the Hothouse that no other business would ever be necessary.

It was a great location, that shop, with big front windows facing onto two big streets because it sat on a prominent corner, an arrowhead of a building shooting right through the heart of the intersection. Now it's a cell phone shop.

My mother went to see Mrs. Kotsopolis at the hospital, asked me if I wanted to go. I didn't. She brought a lemon cake she made from scratch, but they wouldn't let her in.

Every Labor Day I would go fishing with my father, if he were not on duty, and he was rarely on duty because that was our day. It was the one date he actually turned the world over to get away from the job because we decided that was our day—more than Christmas or my birthday—that was not to be broken. Labor Day meant summer was over and I was about to go back to school and so in a meaningful way the calendar was turning over and we were both noticing that. The one Labor Day I remember he did have to work, he wound up saving a kid's life, pulling him out of our very river and squeezing the water right up out of his lungs. It was on the news and everything. Christ, I hated that kid.

It was, and it is, the intake of breath before going back up into the outside world for another year.

"Another year," he said to me, last year, *the* last year, as he cast his line way out over the churning river, in the shadow of Ozzie's Bridge.

"Another year, Dad," I said, doing the same.

"Another step, further out there," he said.

"Out where?"

"Out there," he repeated, without any other signal.

"I guess," I said.

"Soon enough, Russ, you're probably not going to want to do this anymore."

"Don't be stupid," I snapped.

I was really angry, that he said that. But he just laughed at me for being angry, for being a kid.

This year, the first year of *out there*, I wake up to a Labor Day I just want to skip. I feel like while I was sleeping somebody crept in and pressed a bazooka flush against my chest and just blew me out. I feel it, it is nothing there and it is also huge and it is a nothing that hurts brilliant and new like hurt was just concocted.

There is a knock at my door. I can't even recall the last time there was a knock at my door.

It sounds so strange, so foreign and out of place here,

and now I sit up, stupid, staring, working out just exactly what a knock at a door is.

There is another knock, because I am taking too long working it out, so I haul myself over there and open the door with great effort.

DJ is standing there. With a fishing rod.

I should be ecstatic. Any normal person would be ecstatic.

I lose it instead. I am a seventeen-year-old male, a man, a fireman for christsake, and I cannot stop doing what I do not want to do. I want to say hello old friend. I want to say, what a pleasant surprise. I want to slap DJ on the shoulder and talk about stupid frigging fish. I try, actually, to do each of those things, but words don't come out of me and tears do, and I actually cover my mouth and stare at him for a while, silent and mental until it seems like half a day's good fishing has been lost.

DJ is patient. He has always been that.

"Got it together now?" he says as I dig in the back of the closet for my gear.

"Yeah," I say, gesturing for him to lead the way out.

"Good, 'cause if you keep that shit up I'm not going fishing with you."

"Why *are* you going fishing with me?"

"Somebody's got to go with you, right? It's the day.

Labor Day, right? Can't have you sitting around crying
all Labor Day can we?"

"No. We can't have that."

And so we don't. DJ, who never went on these fishing
dates with me and my dad, who never went fishing at all,
as far as I know, who never even ate fish in my company,
turns out to be about the second best fishing companion
you could have. As we sit in the shadow of the amazing
Ozzie's Bridge, it's obvious that he has no more interest in
landing a fish than my dad ever did.

And like with my dad, it is about other stuff.

"Nice spot," he says, casting out into the middle of the
chopping, chipping water.

"Oh, you know this spot," I say, because everyone
knows this spot. We are at the bottom of the stone forty-
foot rise of Ozzie's Bridge, which has stood over this river
for a hundred and fifty years. The strong sunlight cuts this
way and that, through the trees lining the river for miles.
The water moves fast, and there could be fish splashing
everywhere, or none at all.

"Yeah, but I don't know *this spot*," he says to clarify.
"This, right here, is a fine spot."

I cast my line out, further, but the same. We're not
even using bait, or flies.

He means *this spot*. My Dad spot. We are settled on a

big mossy rock the size of a rowboat that extends right out into the river. Just about enough to fit two guys comfortably, close enough, not overclose, fishable, talkable and still just alone enough.

Being alone together. That was how Dad looked at fishing. Organized aloneness. Being in the same place at the same time doing the same thing and doing it alone together. That was us. That is us.

"What happened to us, DJ?" I ask him as the fish practically mock us, jumping and splashing upriver, or not.

The bridge, four big arches in all, insists that you look up at it. I don't fight it.

"A lot of stuff happened to us, Russ."

"Okay, right, but I mean, why did we just—"

"It was probably a lot better fishing with your dad, huh? Probably you'd have pulled in a bunch of fish by now."

I suppose if he doesn't want to talk about himself, or us, he's entitled. I suppose talking about our fathers today is not such a bad thing.

"Sort of. He loved to be here. We loved to both be here, if the weather was nice, together whatever. He was lousy at the actual fishing of fish, however, and that last time, last year, I figured out that he was probably lousy on purpose."

"How did you work that out?"

"Because he caught a fish."

We listen to the rush of the water. The water is really persistent today.

"Finish the story, Russell."

"It was the first and last time he ever caught a fish. Surprised himself half to death when the thing hit his line and when he finally brought it in, DJ, I swear I thought he was going to cry. The way he looked at it . . ."

At this moment, of course, I feel like my dad, looking at that fish, and it takes me some strength to finish this story, but I am going to finish it.

"And I had to take the hook out of the fish's mouth for my dad. And then when we released it and watched it squip away, it was like only then could he even go back to breathing again."

"That's really nice, Russell. That is really very much your dad."

"I know."

"He was a great guy, you know."

Listen to the river, Russ, listen to the river.

"I thought we wouldn't do this," I say.

"I guess we're doing it."

"Your dad was great too, you know that."

"Mmm," DJ says, weak.

Sounds like nothing, right?

"Huh?" I ask.

"I know he was, I know he was. We should just fish now."

"All right," I say, and turn sharpish back the other way, angling myself so DJ is just out of my view. I feel him do likewise as we give our attention completely to the water, to the fresh air, to the sun and the end of the summer and the beginning of what's next.

Until I have to turn back. "DJ, I have to show you something."

He turns to me, waits.

I am wearing a big, loose-fitting button-down shirt that has geek sleeves reaching to the elbow. I place my fishing rod on the ground under my feet and with my right hand push the left sleeve up to the shoulder.

"Christ," DJ says, his expression dead as dead.

It is a tattoo. Fresh enough to still hurt and have a few blistery scabby spots, but brilliant in color and design. It is the exact image of the memorial for our dads they unveiled at the Hothouse. Badges. Eagle. Russ, Dave. Outrageous Courageous.

"Where'd you get that?" he asks flatly.

"Straight from the designer," I say, admiring the thing all over again and feeling even prouder because finally I am showing somebody and it is *the* somebody. "John DeVellis, from the Hothouse. His brother Steven has the tattoo shop in town, did the design for them. John told me just say the word, and I said the damn word before he could even catch his breath. And free, of course. The whole damn thing for free. My mother might kill me when she sees, but I had to have it. Isn't it gorgeous, DJ? You have to go down and—"

"No, thank you." He smoothly pivots on his rock and gets back at the fish.

"DJ, man, you have to—"

"Did I tell you about Melanie? After the party?"

"What? What? No, listen—"

"You want to hear about her? There's loads to tell, no kidding, I'm happy to tell you every bit. . . ."

"No," I snap. "Thanks anyway."

"You sure?" he asks, belligerent.

"I'm sure," I say.

"Okay then, so I guess you just keep your little trophy to yourself, and I'll do the same, huh?"

All I can do is stare at him, my face trying to bridge this gap in ways words appear useless right now.

Unmoved, he just stares back.

Then a dog waggles up in between us on our rock, a houndy, satiny old slobberer doing that thing they do. He visits my face, making me jump, then goes to DJ, fanning me then with his hyperhappy tailworks. DJ pushes him off, but less unfriendly than he handled me.

"I'm sorry, boys," comes the croaky voice behind us.

We both turn to see the old fisher guy, a man I have seen and waved at but that is the extent of knowing him. My dad might have said he was a retired cop. He carries a tackle bag and rod, and stands there in big brown rubber hip waders.

"That's okay," DJ says, the dog having brought him back down, "he's friendly enough."

"I was meaning about the news," the man says. "I was sorry to hear the news. But it's none of your fault, so just don't even give it another thought."

"Okay," I say, puzzled, but, okay.

His dog back under control and on the trail again, the old guy gives us a small salute thing and heads off.

I salute back.

"For godsake, how is it even news anymore?" DJ asks, standing up and just dropping his rod on the ground. "And how would it ever be our fault?" He lets out a small roar of frustration through clenched teeth and starts walking away.

I follow him.

"Come on, DJ, we're not done here," I say, catching up and grabbing his shoulder.

He shakes loose and turns to address me. "Yes we are. I've had enough. And I want to encourage you to let it all go now, too. Okay? Enough is enough. Let go, Russell, move on, grow up, right now, stop commemorating, stop crying. You'll be glad you did."

I open my mouth to argue and like a shot his hand is out and covering my mouth.

"Please, Russell. Ol' pal. No."

He removes his hand from my mouth, and I think we are both satisfied when nothing comes out. He nods, and goes.

I trudge back to the spot, *the* spot, where we were fishing, where the fishing always got done. I can't help looking up and all around, trying to recapture the notion of where, of who, I am. I am looking up at the greatness of Ozzie's Bridge, the immensity of carved stone high over the streaming water. I look up into the trees where the birds call and echo and never leave you as alone as you think you are. But now, unlike before, I am also looking up for who else is around, if there is anybody out there now or am I alone with the river from this point on.

I stand for several minutes on the rock where my father and I fished. I sit down for several more minutes on the rock, where DJ and I fished, the water snapping around me and the rock to get to where it's going. I stand up again, for several more minutes on the rock where we fished, with the water rushing around and past me, and I look all around, and listen, and finally collect up the two fishing rods and make my own way. Away for good from right here.

US AND THEM

The newspaper says Mrs. Helen Kotsopolis's cat, her blue-gray slink of a cat, has been found. He was lying across some of the rubble of the old house he shared with Mrs. Kotsopolis for years and years. They interviewed one neighbor who thought it was twenty years. He had wandered, after the fire, on his own for a remarkable amount of time for a cat his age. If you spread his nine lives over those years, he'd averaged a little over two years per, but by the time he came back and stretched out across the rubble of the house he shared with Mrs. Helen Kotsopolis all that time, he was all out.

I thought it was really something, that a woman was interviewed in the newspaper about the life and death of one slinky blue-gray cat.

Mrs. Helen Kotsopolis's condition remains unchanged.

* * *

"Right," I say when my mother starts telling me about something that sounds like it's supposed to have big meaning. "Board of inquiry, right. There was a board of inquiry."

"It's standard, with the fire department, when there are injuries or fatalities. There is an investigation into what went wrong so that lessons can be learned, to assess whether human error on the part of personnel contributed, or whether the tragedy was unavoidable in the circumstances."

The words may not be amounting to a whole lot for me, but the approach is giving me shivers. This is a lot more than I need on the first day back at school.

"Ma, why are you sounding like somebody off the news while you're right here, talking to me? This is me."

"I know. I know it's you, Russ."

We are sitting over an unusually rich breakfast for a weekday. Waffles, sausages, homemade blueberry muffins and fresh smoothies, likewise produced this very morning in this very kitchen and containing at least eight different ingredients. I know, because I see the peels and pits and cores sitting on the cutting board in front of the blender. I am being extra fortified for something.

"It's ongoing, this inquiry. They are still working on it, might not be finished for a while yet."

"Okay," I say, nibbling carefully, sipping carefully. "Is that it? I mean, you said this is standard procedure."

"Standard."

"Okay, then. Why do you seem so bothered?"

"I just . . . wanted you to know. To be aware. And I want this all to be over. That's all, son. We just need this all to be over. Now. Finally. Just over with and behind us. It's time. And, too, I wanted to make sure you were aware, that it's not quite over yet."

"In that case, you can relax, you've done the job. I am aware. I'm not completely aware of what I am aware *of*, but I am aware. And now I should probably get going, because Adrian is expecting me."

"Of course. Adrian. He's a good friend, isn't he. He's a good guy, Adrian. I'm glad he's your friend."

I get up from the table, wipe my mouth, and haul my stuff to the sink, giving my mother a questioning look all the way.

"Just leave all that there," she says, "I'll take care of that." She's got the time since the private school she teaches in starts a week later than my public one. And since I resent that, I will let her do the cleaning up.

"Cool," I say, then, kissing her on the head I add, "you might want to have a second glass of that smoothie. You don't look all together."

"Thank you," she says. "I think I will. Have a great first day."

It sounds like an order. A gentle one, but an order, still.

The walk to the bus stop is the same old walk. And on my way I pass the same old DJ on the other side of the street, heading for the other bus the other way.

It's not same-old, the way we stand awkwardly on opposite curbs staring across at each other.

"I have your fishing rod," I say. "I'll get it to you."

"No hurry," he says. "I don't fish."

He smiles, so I take it as a joke. I wave, he waves, and we move on.

"So, looking forward to it?" Adrian asks as we bump along on the bus toward a new year.

"Actually," I say, "I am. Been looking forward to it for a while now. Not that school is such a treat, but I just want to, you know, get on with it. You know?"

I turn to face him even though we are a little too close for that sort of thing. But it was one of those statements that, unless you see a guy's face you can't tell if he really gets it.

"I think I know what you mean," he says. "I guess I

would feel pretty much let's-move-on if I had the time you've had. . . ."

"Yeah," I say. "Thanks. And it's not just like, I want to get busy. I also want to get going. We are seniors now. Real life coming. Time to get to work on it for real."

It is clear Adrian has been thinking about this as well, but maybe not in quite the same way as me. "Yeah," he says with a big sigh, "I know."

"You still thinking you want to study to be a vet?"

"Well, yes. But I was thinking I want to make a fool of myself at college for a while first."

"First? *First* you have to get into college. Then you can make a fool of yourself. Then you get to the vet part."

"I know. That's why I have biology honors. Sigh."

We are pulling up at the stop nearest school.

"You thinking more about what you want to do?" he asks me as we get off the bus.

"No," I say.

"No?" he asks, stunned.

"I mean, yes, of course I'm thinking more about it. I'm thinking about it all the time, in fact. But I'm not thinking anything new. I'm a firefighter. I'm going to be a firefighter, you know that."

"Oh," he says, somehow no less stunned. "You're still . . ."

"Of course I'm still . . ." I say. "What kind of a dumb question is that?"

"The dumb kind, I guess," he says, slapping my back good and hard.

It's a funny thing, coming into the school grounds first day of class every September. It's like coming home and leaving home in one move. Because, obviously, we are ending the summer, when we were home all the time and with our families, and going to the kind of institutional world that is the school with its schedules and rules and demands and structure and bosses—both teacher types and students.

But it's also coming home—if your school is half decent which ours just about is—because we are joining up again with mostly the same people we scattered from a couple of months before, who are mostly the same people we joined up with the year before and the year before that. And even if we have been bumping into half of them here and there throughout the summer, when we bump here again at school . . . I don't know, there is something both old hat and special about it at the same time that makes it a tiny bit thrilling.

And it's our last first day. Beginning high school's big

finale. This all blows apart after this. And DJ is right—
rough but right—the time is now to get on with life.

Hanging out, greeting folks in passing, Adrian and
I manage to be about the last to enter the building at
the bell. I feel it when folks give that small extra smile,
the slap across my belly as they pass. I feel it, I understand it, I appreciate it. I file it. We are moving on, in our
ways. Nearly everybody is inside now, headed for the big
assembly that will let the games begin. Adrian and I push
off the wall just as Montgomerie passes in front of us.

Montgomerie is just one of those guys. He's not fat,
but he looks like he is anyway, y'know? His face is kind
of swollen, a little pink, always like he's very stressed
or exhausted by something. He has this white kink of
frizzy hair, and is always wearing clothes that are too
big, as if he buys them anticipating a growth spurt that
doesn't ever arrive.

Montgomerie's father is a cop, and cops and firefighters know each other mostly. Montgomerie's father and
mine knew each other. My dad never liked Montgomerie's dad, and I never liked Montgomerie. We've never
been friends, though we have mostly coexisted peace-
fully enough. We went to the same schools forever, so
there were the early school years when he thought it was

a hoot to make firefighter jokes, about the fire service
being a sort of Little League police department for guys
who weren't tough enough to be cops. That stuff fizzled
out after the time Montgomerie's dad made the papers for
being caught skiing while he was on extended disability
leave. My dad made the papers a few times for stuff like
bravery and service to the community and saving a life or
three and when that happened relations with Montgomerie would worsen for a while but we got through it.

So, as he passes, Montgomerie gives me a smile.

Montgomerie hasn't smiled in my direction since third
grade. And that was only because I threw up my lunch.

You might think under the circumstances, it was a
diplomatic smile. The silent tribute like the others I've
been fielding.

No. It was not that kind of smile.

It's gotten embarrassing now.

*Every year of my life I can remember, since
I was tiny, my father and I have gone to the
ancient department store downtown around
Christmas to get our portrait picture taken, holi-
day style. In the 1960s, I'm sure this was quite
the thing to do, and quite the happenin' place to*

do it. But the place, frankly, is tired now and so, frankly, am I. The department store is on its last legs, decidedly has-been and waiting for somebody with a few bucks and a nice condo idea to come and buy it out of its misery. They still do the whole Christmas display in the windows with trains that don't run anymore and elves that don't wave anymore and a star of Bethlehem that does not lead anybody anywhere anymore because it has turned from white to amber before everybody's jaundiced eyes. It's more depressing than if Christmas were canceled altogether and replaced with a famine or something.

Not in my father's eyes, though.

"It never changes, does it?" he says as we climb up out of the subway to take in all the faded glory.

"If you say so, Dad," I say. I should be doing better, but this year, more than ever, I am having trouble. I am too old for this. I don't want to hurt his feelings, but I sure as hell would like him to catch on on his own. This is not cool. It's not like Ma is surprised anymore, really. And I don't think she'd kill herself if we didn't come home finally without the full ten-print festive selection that

results in nine unused photos and one eight-by-ten mortification for me.

He doesn't catch on, though. Even though we are, really, two very grown men now, he shows no sign that he is ever going to catch on to the lameness of this until the wrecking ball actually shows up passing through our Christmas portrait one fine year.

"Remember the shoes?" he asks.

It's as traditional as Ho Ho Ho.

"I do, of course," I say. I don't strictly remember the shoes because the shoe episode happened when I was about a year and a half old. But I remember the echo of the shoes because he has been retelling me the story faithfully since I was old enough to just about remember the event, so there is an unbroken connection of something like memory.

"You had no good shoes for the picture, not good enough anyway. So we were going to buy some, right here. Only they didn't have any proper picture shoes, not quite, except the one pair . . ."

A little too small.

". . . Just a little too small. Not so small you

couldn't wear them for twenty minutes of photo time. But they would be useless after that . . ."

So we stole them.

"So we stole them, temporarily. Put them right on your little foots, sat for beautiful portraiture, then returned them to the toddlers department with nobody any the wiser."

"Ah, we were sly," I say.

"We were sly," he says. "You need anything this year?"

"My shoes are fine, Dad."

"That doesn't matter. You're hardly going to have your big feet up on the table this time, are you? That shirt, maybe, could be a bit more festive. What do you say, for old time's sake—"

"We are not stealing a shirt, Dad. Not even temporarily."

He couldn't possibly be surprised that I said that. He could not possibly have thought we would do that. But he goes silent, in that way that I know I have hurt his feelings, and I feel bad, trailing after him as the Christmas music plays through the near-empty store and we take the escalator up to the portrait studio.

He has partly bounced back by the time we have navigated through ladies' night wear, to the orphaned little corner where the studio hangs on.

"You behave in here now," he says at the same time the photographer lady sees us and smiles hard. In my mind she is laughing at us, probably in hers too, but certainly not in Dad's. "You behave. Any fussing and there will be no root beer float downstairs afterward."

God, no, the root beer float, at the ancient fountain, where the original Tarzan from the movies was supposed to have brought Cheeta for a burger and milkshake on a promotional visit. It was in the papers, they say.

He never catches on. I don't want a root beer float. Why does he never catch on?

"I'll behave, Dad," I say. "No fussin'."

Gathered up in the gym, the school feels densely populated. And sweaty. Though there are only maybe two hundred and fifty kids in senior year all together and they are all cleaner than they will probably be at any other moment this year, the gym just always retains that overly close feel. Sometimes that's not so bad, in a tight community type of way.

Other times, it can feel like it's closing in on you.

There are photos up there on the stage. Hero photos up next to the flag at the back of the stage, in the corner. They aren't huge, but big enough to know that it's a couple of firefighters, in uniform, in official hero-type portraits. My heart leaps at the sight of my dad and DJ's dad up there on display for everybody and I tell you, if my heart leaps any more than it has leapt over the last month it's going either to the heart Olympics or the morgue.

Somebody pats me on the back and I don't know who and I don't want to know who. They mean well. They always mean well. Everybody means well and everybody is trying to be good and everybody just wants to pay respects but at this point I've been paid so much I must owe people change.

No mention is made of the heroes behind the principal the whole time she talks. She talks about renewal and new years and new beginnings and new challenges and new opportunities. I can't stop staring at the pictures, even though I already know them so well. I just don't know them *there*. But now it's as if they have always been there and are just part of the fabric of life here and, well, the school and the principal and the students and everybody just owns them now.

Like everything else, we will get used to this.

I don't know why, but I am clapping. Everybody is clapping, which is probably the best explanation for why I am clapping, but the words we just heard have not really added up to anything in my brain other than the thought that I am glad it is over and I am hugely happy to be filing off in the direction of my homeroom classroom. Followed by English and Spanish and math and my face happy to be stuck in a textbook no different from every other face.

Montgomerie gets "friendlier" as the first week rolls on. He smiles more and the smiling leads to smirking and the smirking leads to uninvited chatting.

"Inquiring minds want to know," he says to greet the day on Friday morning in the school yard.

I have no clue what he's talking about and no interest in finding out. "Well yeah," I say, "I guess they do. That's what makes them inquiring."

"Yeah, well right now they are inquiring about phony heroes."

I said before I was going to have to get re-used to that hero word so I could hear it without going all wobbly. Now, it's whacking me again only right away it feels different, wicked. I get a chill, then hot.

"What are you talking about?" I say as guys start gathering around us immediately. They always know.

"I'm talking about a hero's not a hero if he's so off his face he can't do his job. I'm talking about maybe a hero is more like a criminal if some old lady maybe dies because the firemen who were supposed to save her were too busy partying."

Here is a phrase I never fully understood until right this minute: *in cold blood.* It feels exactly like that now, as I try and digest what Montgomerie is saying at me, my mind working to make sense of it while my guts are way ahead and already know how to feel.

"Montgomerie," I say as slow and low as I can get it, "this is the only thing I am going to say about this, to you, ever: Withdraw that statement. Right now."

"Sorry to tell you, but it's the truth. I happen to know there was a board of inquiry, and they found out that your father and DJ's father were wasted that night. Sorry. Truth hurts, man. But what I know now everybody's gonna know soon enough, and this whole big lie is gonna be over."

I breathe in deep. I know some people are screwed up and will say anything and I will need to learn to deal with it. I want myself under control, I want that for me, and I will have that.

I am practically standing on his shoes, breathing his rancid air. I can feel my whole body shaking but I try desperately to keep it from showing to the whole, large assembled crowd. "Last warning. First, you are going to take that back. Then, you are going to shut your fat face. Or I swear, I'm going to kill you."

"Runs in the family, I guess. Murder incorporated."

Because I have great friends it's like a real riot. Everybody swarms and swings and pushes forward at once, several people rushing to just separate us but the majority going after Montgomerie. Adrian's in there, Cameron, Burgess . . .

I don't even feel my body do anything, don't know if I have jumped, dived or flown, but I am kneeling on Montgomerie's chest, with one hand squeezing his throat and the other covering his face like a claw, and I am bouncing his skull hard enough off the ground, I actually hyperextend my elbow and lose half my strength. Half is enough, though, because I can still manage to bounce his head seven, eight, nine times, making a thunk sound come out the back and a strangled whine sound come out the front until my friends drag me off and toward the school as the authorities are coming.

As we are scuttling in, my phone goes off in my pocket. There is a text.

I think you should come home, my mother has written.

I get instantly nauseous with dread, uncertainty. Certainty.

"I have to go," I say, yanking away from them.

"Dad. What are we doing? I don't want to go."

"You might not know what you want. It's a father's job, maybe about his biggest job, to help his boy get to the place where he knows what he wants."

I know I don't want to be in the place I am in right now, which is in the car speeding up Route 95 North. It is an unplanned trip. So unplanned we never even discussed it. So unplanned my mother at work doesn't even know we're making it. So unplanned I am still about one-quarter asleep and we haven't even bothered to do our breakfast thing.

"Breakfast on the road will be part of the fun," he says.

"You keep driving like this and we will be part of the road," I say. *Other cars appear to be reversing past our windows.* *"What is the rush, anyway?"*

"We are making up for lost time, Russell."

"Well, wasting time is the same as losing time, Dad, and this is a great waste of time. I have no interest in going to college. You know that, I know that, everybody who knows me knows that. What is the point of going to 'visit' a college I am never going to see again?"

He speeds up.

"Slow down," I snap.

He slows down.

"You need to keep your options open," he says.

"I'm a firefighter. I have always been one and I will always be one. We have been talking about this forever. We will work together someday. Turn the car around and go make me breakfast, ya loon."

A smile spreads across the old man's face, but it doesn't quite settle me. It's nervous and unsure. Apologetic.

"You might not want to do with your life what I'm doing with mine," he says softly. "That's all I'm saying. It was wrong not to get you to at least look at the possibilities out there, before you commit your whole future. . . ."

"No," I say calmly, looking away from him to

the flashing road markings. "That's why I had the day off, remember? I didn't need the 'college open day,' because I'm not going to college."

He has gradually speeded up. The white markings are like one blurry slash now, and they are running right under us, splitting the car down the middle between us.

"I thought about going here when I was your age," he says. "Russ, it's a beautiful place, you won't believe it. It's a whole different . . . life is different here. Maybe you'll go, get your degree, you can still think about the fire service. . . ."

"Why didn't we talk about this before?" I ask.

"It just occurred to me," he says, clearly now looking off into the distance, onto the campus, into my future.

"Get in your lane, Dad," I say. "And slow down."

"Oh, hell," he says, and doesn't need to say more. I see the blue lights bouncing off the mirrors. Dad quickly reaches up and checks that the cloth fire department shoulder patch is up on the dash where he keeps it.

It takes a full mile to properly come to a stop,

as Dad is going too fast and doesn't take the direct-est route to the breakdown lane. By the time the state trooper gets to the driver's side window, he already sounds almost disgusted.

"What on earth would somebody need to be driving that fast for at this time of the morning? Are you going to tell me you are two hours late for work"—he leans in to check me out—"and it's take-your-son-to-work day?"

Dad laughs, a guilty-sounding cackle of a thing I would be happy never to hear again. "No, sir," he says. "I was just taking my son for his college visit, and I guess we were getting a little excited, talking about his future and everything and I just failed to watch my speed—"

"Or your lane," the officer snaps.

This feels very bad.

Dad cackles. I'd really rather see him hauled in than resort to that laugh.

"Yes, sorry about all that. But, no, work had nothing to do with it. Work's back that way." He thumbs back in the direction of home and with his other hand taps the dashboard where the FD patch is.

The trooper leans over the windshield to inspect closely.

"That badge yours?" he says, back at Dad's window.

"Yes, sir, it is."

He stares hard at Dad for half a minute. I can only guess what my father feels but I could honestly wet myself right now.

"What's your station?" the cop asks.

Dad gives him the station's official designated number.

"The Hothouse?" Mr. State Trooper says almost incredulously. "Sir, you are stationed at the Hothouse?"

"Yes, sir," Dad says, something like his regular voice coming back into play. You can hear his vocal cords slacken.

"Dammit, man, you work for Jim Clerk? Jim Clerk is your boss?"

It would appear things have taken a turn for the unincarcerated.

"That's my boss, yes, sir. No better man alive, is there?"

"No, there certainly isn't. You are a lucky man."

"I know I am."

"You probably don't know how lucky. Listen. Dammit, Jim Clerk . . ." He shakes his head and smiles at whatever wondrous things Jim Clerk has done for him, his village, his people and their pets and wildlife. "Listen, I am going to send you on your way . . ."

The cop has now leaned in a little bit closer. He sniffs Dad. Then he pauses, processes. He looks really hard at the driver's eyes.

"You got ten more miles to the college. They have fine coffee. Enjoy it throughout your tour."

Dad knows an order when he hears one. "I will. Thanks."

And, like that. Like that, we are out of the breakdown lane, back on the road, zipping only a couple mph over the speed limit toward the college.

"Now, where were we?" Dad asks, happily enough that the whole episode may have already been deleted. "Breakfast? Were we talking about stopping for breakfast?"

I am staring at him, and I know I look like a dummy because I am breathing a little heavy out my mouth. I turn away from him to stare

out my window and I am not certain I would be
less happy if the public servant had done his job
instead of being a good old boy.
    "I couldn't eat right now," I say.

My mother is on the couch and already speaking fast as I walk into the living room.

"Firstly, these were just premature leaks, and the actual Board of Inquiry did not release anything until somebody started saying things to the press, and so they rushed out the report. And the fire department does not want to say—"

"Ma," I say firmly enough to stop her short. "I just need you to tell me if it's true. I need to know what's true. Is it true?"

She shifts her position on the couch from left-facing to right and back again. She is staring at me with wide and scared eyes. But there is more nervousness to her than shock or even surprise.

She takes a deep inhale that nearly pulls me closer to her.

"Your dad was in a lot of pain, Russell. Pain that was a direct result of how much of himself he put into that *infernal* job." Her anger is real and intense there and when she hits the word *infernal* it sounds like a car engine idling then suddenly you stomp the gas pedal. "And *this* is what they do to him."

"What about the pain?" I ask. "What does that mean?"

"He took medication, for the pain, Russ. It's how he got through it."

My mind is running around the monstrous maze of this situation, trying to find a way through. This, looks like a way through.

"So? What's wrong with that? There's nothing wrong with that. We see it in sports all the time, they give them something for the pain and they are back on the field. That's what tough guys do, right? They can't say, just because he took pain medication. . . ."

"He may have taken a lot, of medication," she says. "He may have taken too much."

I hear the sound of every opening in the maze slapping shut. Nothing but walls.

"Are you saying, Ma, that he *did* take too much?"

"Russell, the department says that they are not concluding anything until every scrap of detail has been reexamined. . . ."

"That's good. But are you saying that he *did* take too much? Are you saying, Ma," I say, and this time it is my turn to take a deep vacuum of an inhale that removes all the air from the room, "that you *know* that he took too much?"

We sit looking at each other for a few long seconds. We are looking at each other in a way we have never quite looked at each other before, and probably that is our life now.

"I do not *know* that, Russell."

That was not the best answer.

The phone rings and rings until my mother unplugs it. Newspeople want to talk to her, and maybe to me, about my father.

I don't feel like talking to anybody about my father just now.

When I start coming out of the trance-thing that has taken me over, I realize I am sitting in a tub of cold water.

"What did the board say about DJ's father?" I ask. I am standing in the doorway of my mother's bedroom. My parents' bedroom. My mother's bedroom. I am standing in my old slippers, which I found at the back of my closet. I am wearing my pale blue-and-white striped flannel pajamas, which reach just above my ankles and just above my wrists. I'm wearing my thick velour bathrobe that no longer has its sash. I am shaking like a machine gun with bone-cold and everything else.

"They said he was a fine firefighter and a hero," she says, waving me over to the bed.

I sit on the bed beside her and allow her to wrap me up tight in her arms. Though I keep my own arms down at my sides.

"What else did they say?" I ask.

"They said they will stand behind him completely until all the facts have been double and triple verified and—"

"Ma?"

"Right," she says. And she tells me.

All firefighters are in pain. Of one kind or another, and usually several kinds at once. They get hurt a lot. The work is dangerous, the training is dangerous, and the exercise they do to keep in shape for all that is tough so even the training for the training is dangerous. They hurt when they don't see their families for days at a time. They hurt when they fight a particularly nasty fire for six hours and what is left at the end of it is an icy smoking stink pile of somebody's home or church or restaurant. Or worse. When that happens, they take the pain with them for days, for months, for ever.

I knew this, a little bit. I would know if he was limping. I would know if he was grouchy or if he seemed to need a little more sleep than usual or if he seemed to get frustrated over not much and my mother would rustle me away to give him space. I didn't like it, but I found it funny when she gave it a name. The Russell Rustle, made it seem more of a game, more about me, since it had my name on it.

But really, there was no one thing in my dad's life that displeased him, specifically. I know he loved me and my mom. I know that. I know it. I know he loved his work and he loved fishless fishing and he loved playing fiddle pretty badly because I have a mental picture album in my head of him smiling broadly at all those things over and over. But I notice, as I flip through that album, a lot of pictures of him not smiling. Just flatline, over nothing anybody seems to know. Only I did know, a little.

I knew that as happy and sweet a man as he was, there was a particle of him that was unreasonable with the rest of him, not in agreement with the bright and shiny rest of him, at the same time.

Ma had a name for that one too because my mom developed a gift for this kind of thing. The Jolly Melancholy, is what she called it.

And just like the Russell Rustle, the Jolly Melancholy was one of her perfect contradiction phrases that made me feel all right about something that I might not otherwise have been all right about. Something that was, it turns out, not at all all right.

Something I will never feel all right about again.

And much as they are the same, much as they are brothers and their own breed, team, planet, whatever they want to call themselves, they all do their own little and big things, by themselves, to deal with the pain and fear and boredom and anger that come with the life.

There is one guy who works at the Hothouse, he uses every single spare moment at the station lifting weights. My dad told me lots of days the guy skipped sleep for working out. He enters bodybuilding contests. He had his shirt off at the cookout. He looks like bookshelves that can walk. Another guy spends hundreds of hours producing a quarterly magazine on beekeeping that he gets printed all nice at a printer's. Dad said the most bee thing about *The Quarterly Bee* was the buzzing sound all over the Hothouse when everybody fell asleep at once reading the thing. Lots of them are boxers or martial arts guys.

The Board of Inquiry says Dad, and Dad's best friend, were a different story.

. . . and with all investigations now concluded, the Board has accepted the facts as stated in the original report. The two firefighters who died in the blaze were the first ones into the kitchen on the second floor of the structure. That both went in without either masks or radios. That they were quickly overcome by smoke and heat and became disoriented. They attempted to navigate their way out of the situation by using hose as a guideline as one led the other. But in their disorientation had followed the hose in the wrong direction, farther into the fire. When the explosion occurred they would not have stood any chance of escaping the full force.

While toxicology reports revealed significant levels of prescription drugs in one man and illegal drugs in the other, as well as alcohol in both their systems, the Board could not conclude if this contributed to their deaths.

"We aren't going to just take it, are we?" I ask DJ.

I am standing on his porch with the two fishing rods in my hands. I know that what I look like is the guy in the famous painting standing expressionless with his wife and his pitchfork. But what I feel is defiant.

"I think we are," he says as flatly as that pitchfork

guy would have said it.

"We can do something about this, DJ," I say. "We have to straighten this out. We can, you and I, as a team. Life is a team sport, right?"

"Nice," he says. "I mean, definitely corny, but nice."

"My dad always said that."

"I remember. Your dad was corny."

"He was," I say happily. Sadly. "He was corny. He was true-blue corny. How could people not know that? Only the best people are corny."

"It would be good if people could just shut up about them now, you know?"

"They should. They should shut up. You know what I loved? I loved when my dad would come home late at night and we would cook stuff. Whatever was there, we would just cook stuff, just to have it, just to do it. People don't know about this kind of stuff. Great things. One of the . . . last times, y'know, it was really late and there was practically nothing, but he was gonna do it anyway. And he made us nachos. Even though we didn't have nacho chips but we had had Chinese food the day before so he tried to make nachos out of these shrimp chips that were there, and he pours hot cheese over them and they just dissolved and fizzled as if we were melting plastic wrap on the stove. We didn't eat, but we laughed a whole bunch. We laughed a whole bunch, and people don't know anything about that kind of thing."

DJ laughs too, for a few seconds and then something a little sadder comes over his face and he looks just a bit sorry for me.

"I'm not going fishing, Russell," he says.

"The Board of Inquiry is wrong, DJ," I say.

He is not budging from his doorway. And I am not budging with the fishing rods.

"I remember one four-day-off shift," he says after a while, "when my dad built me an entire fort for my army men because he thought I wanted one, which I didn't. But then on the second day he tripped and fell on it and it was like one of those Midwest tornado-wrecked houses, broken into more pieces than before he built it in the first place. Then, by the time he finally went back to work two days later the whole thing was built again. He had spent his whole four-day shift on dollhouse duty. I loved it, then. Then, it had become something."

"You still love it now. I bet it's still in your room. You think he did it all on purpose, falling on it and rebuilding it, to get you to love it?"

It was meant as a joke.

"No," he says, staring at the silvery hook dangling off one fishing line as if he is entranced. "I think he smashed it in a fit when he saw I didn't really want it. Then he rebuilt it because he felt bad."

"Oh," I say. "Anyway, it worked, huh?"

"When I saw the furniture and the army guys inside, and all the obvious repairs, how could I not . . ." His voice trails off, before he pulls it back up again. "But then, later, I figured it was all because he just fell on the damn thing and that's what broke it."

"But you see, DJ, that's it, that's the thing. Nobody knew them the way we did and that's why you and I are the ones to put this all right. This stuff they are saying about our dads is not true, and we will prove it's not true. We'll—"

"No, we won't," he says crisply.

"What are you talking about? We certainly will. Why wouldn't we?"

He stares at me, like I'm supposed to work it out for myself. Then he practically spits like he's angry that I can't.

"Because the board is right."

"They are *not* right," I snap. "What's gotten into you? Why are you being like this?"

His two hands are pressed against either side of the doorway like he is Samson trying to break the building apart. He lets his head hang down in a way I cannot see his face, a pose I don't like at all.

"DJ?"

He brings his eyes up to face me in a way I don't like any better.

"I have known for some time now what my dad was like, Russell. That's, pretty much, why I couldn't face you anymore. My father was a mess, and I knew it. And it was humiliating, especially because I still thought your dad was a hero."

"My dad *was* a hero!" I shout. "He still is."

He remains calm, or something that looks like calm but isn't at all.

"They are right, Russ. Everybody is right. They weren't heroes, they were losers. And the sooner we let it go, the sooner it will just be over with."

"Go to hell," I say, just as fake calmly.

"They should have left us alone a long time ago," he says. "They should have left us alone with what was ours, but they wanted it to be theirs because they all needed big phony heroes for themselves. I bet they leave us alone now."

"I'll leave you alone now," I say, throw one fishing rod down on the porch and stomp off.

"That's probably a good idea," he says.

It feels like a trial. Two defendants sitting at trial except only one of us is here.

Nobody is doing anything wrong. Nobody is even saying anything. Maybe that's a big part of the problem. The atmosphere in the classroom feels cold and stiff even if it is my imagination.

It is not my imagination. But maybe I am partly responsible for the way it feels. I know from my rigidity, my silence, my unrecognizable expression and even more unrecognizable folded hands that I have brought tension and uncertainty to the classroom just by being here.

But what do they want? Would they rather I leave? Or just stay home in the first place until everything blows over? When will that be? Can somebody tell me? Because I would really, really like to know, and I have never been in this situation before. I have never even heard of anybody in this situation before.

Montgomerie hasn't said a word to me, hasn't so much as glanced in my direction. Not a smirk. Almost respectful. You'd have to think this was a good thing, wouldn't you?

Something's got to happen today, though, because we have a visitor scheduled. We have a representative of the fire department coming to speak to us today.

The school requested it. The school needs this put right or at least put neat because everybody recognizes how unbearable it is. The papers and radio and all the other news has not been nice. It's not saying huge monstrous things—yet—but it is not hero talk like it was before, I can tell you that. My mother has quietly rolled out a news blackout in the house, just short of taping the windows over, but there is no avoiding it because it seeps under and around whatever you do, like smoke.

So we have a visitor. He is coming to speak to our modest homeroom class personally first, followed by a more general address to the school in the gym. And it's someone we can trust to know what's what because it is the big guy, Jim Clerk, coming to lay it all smooth for us.

Which, now, is making things more tense. If you tried to lift me out of my seat right now I would have all the flexibility of a garden gnome.

But after an excruciating silent wait, the bell rings for us to get up and go to our first class, which is supposed to be gym. Mr. Clerk was to be here by now, and everybody kind of squirms, looks around, half spilling out of seats but hanging on at the same time. Then, just as we are about to go, Mrs. Boyd waves us back down.

"I believe our special guest is here," she says, more in relief than actual gladness. She scurries to the door to let him in.

It isn't him.

It is a representative of the fire department, sure. In fact, it's three representatives.

Two young guys, firefighters, but so new they have mustaches that could lose a competition with mine, come strolling in in full gear, with axes and masks and everything. Tailing politely behind them is a dog. A dalmatian.

"Okay, students," a clearly confused but unfailingly polite Mrs. Boyd says, "now please give your full attention to these men . . . who have come here to . . . tell us all about life as firefighters."

What? I know this presentation inside out. It's the professional-day schtick.

My dad and DJ's used to do this a lot of years ago. They practiced in our living room.

Where is Jim Clerk? Where is our reassuring talk about what really matters? Telling us *all about life as fire-fighters*?

My pose is rigid no more.

"I already know all about the lives of firefighters," I say, smacking the top of my desk as I shove out of my seat.

"Please, Russell," Mrs. Boyd says, but it is obvious who is in charge now and it is not Mrs. Boyd. "Please, take your seat."

I am rolling up my sleeve as I roll up the aisle. "See this, Mrs. Boyd," I say, pausing and poking my own sore tattooed arm, "I've already had the 'lives of firefighters' lesson and here's my badge, okay?" I don't really wait for her okay. I am still flashing the tattoo when I pass the fire boys. They stare pretty good.

I don't look back as I storm out the door.

I'm a block up the road when Adrian catches up to me.

"If you are supposed to haul me back, you're making a mistake," I point out.

"I wasn't told specifically what I was supposed to be doing, other than to go after you."

"That what you're doing?"

"I guess it is."

"Well you can escort me where I'm going, but you're not coming inside."

"And that's to the Hothouse, isn't it."

"Damn right it is."

We march side by side with great purpose, almost

military. The solidarity, I have to say, feels like blood being pumped into my sad body after having so much of it bled out of me.

"Thanks, man," I say to Adrian as I deposit him there on the sidewalk outside the Hothouse.

"Y'know, whatever, your dad is still to me a total beast hero," he says. "Always will be."

"And to everybody else? What's everybody else saying, Adrian?"

He stares, I stare. He opens his mouth to speak, and I just about stick my pointer finger right in there.

"It's gotta be true, Adrian. I mean thanks and everything, but whatever comes out of your mouth next has got to be true because one more particle of bullshit is going to blow the world up."

I pull back and wait.

Adrian nods at me, and shuts his mouth.

I turn right away from him, because I have a job to do and I have to be able to stand up and I feel strength seeping out of me by the second.

"Jim Clerk," I call out, standing up, but still so small in between the two big machines, engine and ladder. "Jim Clerk!"

I had forgotten, totally, absolutely, how much I loved

this place. The gleaming machines, the size and scale of the place, the smell of the guys, which is with you no matter where you go. The hoses and axes and endless array of cleaning products and gadgets which always, always suggested to me that this was the place in the universe that was more dedicated than any other to the ideal of doing important, heroic stuff, doing it right, keeping things right. I still remember out there at the farthest reach of my memory, coming in here the first time with my dad and being convinced beyond all reason that this place was what heaven must be. Only better, because heaven didn't need heroics, and this place demanded it.

I cannot believe how soon all that was wiped off my board.

Jim comes out of his office.

"Shouldn't you be in school right now?" he asks.

"Shouldn't *you* be in my school right now?" I answer.

"As I'm sure you can understand, Russell, I am extraordinarily busy right now."

"That's the thing. That's exactly the thing, you see. I don't understand. I don't understand. Why won't you stop it, Mr. Clerk? Can't you just make it all stop, right now and for good?"

He lets out a great sigh and with Jim Clerk's voice even a sigh is something that reassures you and calms you right down.

Unless you are here and now.

"Is that your answer?"

"No," he says patiently. "I apologize. I just want to say the right words. Please understand, I am doing what I can. But I can't force things. The different investigations have to be allowed to run their course in order for people to have confidence in the results. Don't you worry. The fact of the matter is that both your dads were heroes and will continue to be heroes in the eyes of everybody who appreciates what we do, no matter what happens. Great men are great men, and nothing can alter—"

"Is that what I think it is?" I say, as my eye drifts past Jim, to the wall beyond.

"Oh," he says, brightening up at being able to get off the subject. Sort of. "It is of course. They did a great job, didn't they? Fitting, and beautiful?"

He leads me to that back wall, where the shiny new tribute sits.

Sits. Propped against the wall in front of the two great beastly machines.

"Yeah," I say, "it's beautiful. But I thought it was going

to hang in some big open conspicuous spot, a place of honor, like."

"The thing is," Jim says, putting a hand on my shoulder as we admire Dad's badge together, "with things the way they are right now, it was decided that anything showy would not be appropriate, at this time." His voice gets smaller, slower, and a little less reassuring toward the tail end there. Then it comes all the way back. "But the guys, oh, I'll tell you, the love and devotion in this house for your fathers, is an overwhelming thing. The guys wanted to have that thing up, and there was no two ways about it, so we have our own small quiet thing here. It's temporary."

"Your own?" I say, like he has said something in Russian. "Your *own*, quiet, thing?"

"Don't you worry, though. There will be something a little more prominent down the line. . . ."

I don't say anything to that. I nod, even. But I feel my tight fists bouncing lightly off my thighs. "Thank you, Jim," I say, and start walking out.

I repeat the thanks, walk more slowly. I look back at the big shiny tribute sitting on the floor. If one of those young kid firefighters drives the ladder truck a couple of feet too far, the thing is smashed. I walk between the world's shiningest trucks, touching them, sorry about the fingerprints but unable to not touch. I look up and around and around again, turning and walking until I am a bit dizzy walking out into the sun.

"You okay?" Adrian says, steadying me with a flat palm on my chest.

I wait a bit, think a bit.

"Of course I am," I say. "I'm a fireman. We can take it. Whatever it is, we can take it."

I turn and go back to Big Jim.

"Jim," I say as big as I can be, "I want that." I point at it.

There is no discussion.

BURNT OFFERINGS

Life is a team sport, son, is what my dad told me over and over and over again.

Is it, though? Is it a team? Was it a team? What is a team, in the end?

Who is your team?

Who is mine?

I am staring at my computer, at today's edition of the paper, and yesterday's, and parts of tomorrow's as it is being assembled because that's the beauty, isn't it, of the electronic paper, that you can watch all the new elements fly right up onto the screen and stick there, stick right onto the story, just as fast as it all comes in. And then you get to watch as people digest and regurgitate the story and let you all know what they think about the story even if they haven't had enough time to give the story a proper think. You almost don't want to look away to grab a peanut or wash your hot face because you might miss the next micro-development of the story and two thousand people's well-considered instantaneous reaction to it. It is a beautiful thing to watch the construction of it all in 3-D, not to mention dimensions you never even asked for.

"How could nobody know?" I ask, stomping into my mother's bedroom feeling the heat rise off of me. "Ma? About these guys? How could nobody know, with how close they were with each other. With everybody. Is that even possible, that nobody could know?"

She stares at me now, with the old-fashioned slow-mo newspaper folded in her lap, on top of the blankets. Her lips are slightly parted like she is going to tell me something but she's not telling me anything.

"For godsake, DJ knew. About his own dad. How could DJ know and everybody else not?"

Suddenly she starts poring over the newspaper as if the answer is in there, then just as suddenly she comes out with, "A lot of times, Russ, we allow ourselves to believe what we would like to be true, even if that truth is unlikely. A lot of times we can maintain the truth we need until we are made to see something else by force."

She does not look up from the paper as she says this. The radio, pulled off the night table and lying on the bed beside her, is playing soft jazz music now, but the room is filled with a mammoth silence anyway.

I return to the room, the net, the news. The site, the comments section that follows the toxicology report article, is filling up fast.

The message board is alight.

. . . pair of disgraces . . .

If only they were still alive . . . so they could be shot. . . .

I feel sorry for the families. The humiliation worse than death.

How about the poor old woman?

Heads should roll.

Somebody's got to pay. Got to pay.

Mrs. Kotsopolis taught me in school . . . a wonderful, gentle soul. . . .

Their names shall live in infamy. . . .

That is the voice of the city, right there. That is everybody speaking, right there.

I want to cut my wrists. I want to go to the park, and soak myself in gasoline, and make a brilliant bonfire of myself. What are they called in China? Burnt offerings.

Holy shit. Holy shit. Jesus. My God. God help me.

I am on my knees, by no effort of my own. It is as if I

have been thrown right to the floor, by the power of those words from all those people, and they just keep coming. I am on my knees, leaning on the edge of the desk, just about holding myself upright, and still, still, holding down the key that is scrolling the words, the endless deathless hateful cascade of words directed toward the memory of my father. And I cannot stop reading. I'm like a body, electrocuted on a high voltage wire, tangled and unable to even fall off the charge.

He was such a good man, my dad. He made me pancakes with faces on them, and a fire helmet on top traced out of red licorice. He saved that lucky little puke of a drowned kid. He did more selfless things in a month than every last one of these poster jerks have probably done in their whole cowardly lives.

But I agree with them on this one thing: if he were here now I'd kill him myself. What did you go and do, Dad?

How did nobody know about the other stuff? How did nobody know? How did they not stop him?

How did I not know?

I am still on my knees.

It's only his first time ever in the hospital overnight. That's what he says.

"Well, that's the truth for all the time I've known him, and that's a damn long time." Russell is talking. Big Russell. He is taking DJ and me to visit my dad in the hospital after his surgery. Dad broke up his ankle pretty comprehensively when the guys were fighting a routine enough fire on the first floor around the back of a triple-decker.

"You can never, never relax," Russell is saying, to us, to himself, to my dad even though we're not there yet. We are in the hospital, walking up the stairs to Dad's floor. "It was my fault, it was everybody's fault. We're thinking it's a little baby-ass fire and we're hosing on it like we're pissin' in a flower bed, joking about what a shame the fire didn't successfully gut this crappy house. . . ."

And the porches fell off. Just like that, like somebody came by with a great invisible cake knife and separated the triple-decker house from its triple-decker porches and down they came collapsing on themselves and then on my dad.

"And he almost got away, too. Everybody managed to jump straight back in time, and your dad, who was closest to the house to begin with, *almost made it but the damn thing caught his leg like an alligator snatching a dog off a canal bank."*

We are on his floor now, but we are off visiting hours. Way off. I visited this afternoon with my mother, during normal hours, but Dad was quite groggy. And anyway, Russell said we needed a man trip, a proper guys-only visit.

"He screamed and cried like a baby, I'll tell ya," Russell says as we near the nurses' station. "It was very embarrassing for the rest of the guys."

"He did?" Both DJ and I gasp.

Russell keeps walking down the corridor, but walks backward as he grins at us. "Dave? Your dad? Your goddad? My David? Not in this lifetime, children. You could pull that man's damn head off, and if you listened real close you just might get a teeny small ouch. More likely he'd just say, Hey, pop my damn head back on."

It is with great relief we receive that clarification.

It's what I already knew anyway, but it's good not to have it blown apart.

"How are ya, love?" Russell says to the nurse on duty.

"*You know the rules,*" *she says. It is eleven forty-five p.m.*

"*I do indeed,*" *he says sweetly.* "*Is our hero awake?*"

"*All of our heroes are going to be awake if you do not lower your voice.*"

"*Sorry,*" *he says, and points silently in the direction of Dad's room, shuffling little baby steps in that direction. It's like he's playing a game of charades, and he's been assigned the word* impish.

"*Check that, boys,*" *Russell says quietly as we approach Dad's door.* "*You see the way it is? Keys to the city, our own whole set of alternative rules, that's what the likes of me and this guy in here have. People appreciate us. People love us. 'Cause we earn it. Remember that. Proud?*"

"*Proud,*" *I say, quick and snappy like a little kid.*

"*Embarrassed,*" *DJ says, but he says it with a slanty grin. Looks just like his dad.*

"*Hey,*" *Dad says when he sees us slip in. He gives us a big wave and a groggy beaming smile. He is in a double room, but the other bed is empty.*

"*Do it hurt?*" *Russell asks, leaning in to hug Dad.*

"Well," Dad says, "the ankle hurts like hell, down there. But by the time it travels up here"—he taps the side of his head—"the pain seems to have lost its way."

"I see," Russell says, pinging a finger against Dad's intravenous drip. "Here, let's confuse it a little more for good measure."

He pulls a square flat bottle of spiced rum out of his back pocket.

"Should those things be mixed, actually?" DJ asks.

His father turns a look on him, eyebrows to the ceiling. "Perhaps there is a party elsewhere you need to be pooping?"

DJ shrugs.

"Ah," Dad says happily, but wearily. He takes the bottle and unscrews the cap. "It's only a pint. Not sure how long I can last though, to be honest." He takes a sip.

He makes another big sizzly ahhh sound. Russell reaches for the bottle, but Dad yanks it away.

"Wrong Russ," he says, waving me over.

I feel like I have been knighted or something.

My face goes blush-hot. I go up to him, and he hugs me, grabs the back of my head hard, and pulls my cheek to his bristly cheek.

Then I take my sip.

If I lit ten stick matches and then swallowed them all together while they were still lit, that would be approximately this feeling.

I make a face, a failed smile with a grimace that must make me look like a doctor's office skull. But the men don't laugh at me. I pass the bottle to DJ, who raises it like a salute to my dad, then takes his sip.

He makes the doctor's office skull face.

The room is very warm all over. The men drink, then drink again, their faces speaking of butterscotch and warm hot chocolate and there does not appear to be pain in the mix anywhere.

We pass the bottle around evenly. Dad seems to waft in and out of sleep, but even when his eyes are closed he is smiling a smile of understanding, and every time his eyes pop open again they pop right on me.

"This is kind of fun," DJ says after his third touch of the bottle.

"Yeah, Dad," I say, "you should get hurt more often."

"I am planning to," he says as he drifts off for the last time tonight, still grinning contentment.

Dad got hurt more often over time, so I got to know the hospital fairly well. County is not renowned for heart surgery or plastic surgery or solving anything previously unsolvable, so we don't attract a lot of big-name patients. *Big-name* around here almost exclusively refers to the reason that got you admitted, rather than anything that happens to you once you check in.

There is one big name in our hospital now. Helen Kotsopolis.

And I have to see her. I have to tell her I am sorry, because I am, and apologize for my family. And beyond that, I have to tell her how sorry my dad is. Because I know he is. I know how sorry he is, and I know he needs me to do this as much as she needs to be told. Mrs. Kotsopolis can forgive him or not, she can slap my face red raw and I will stand there and take it for as long as necessary, but I have to go in.

Finding somebody in County is not the hardest thing in the world, so I expect to locate Mrs. Kotsopolis's room quickly. I stop first in the gift shop, across from the dining room on the first floor. It's only about eight by twelve feet and has the same collection of spirit boosters they probably carry in every hospital—candy, teddy bears, paperbacks. But I am surprised to find that they carry one of the biggest selections of watches I have seen outside of a jewelry store. They are all propped up nice, too, in this elevated, lighted case that serves as a partial wall between the gift shop and the main corridor. Men's watches, ladies' watches, pocket watches, tiny tabletop clocks with exposed works that twist this way and that and catch even more of that strong, too-strong hospital light.

"Why so many watches?" I ask the older lady who has come from behind the counter to dust right in front of me. There's not even any dust here. She thought I was going to steal something, more like.

"Those are our big fund-raiser," she says. "County Volunteers Organization takes donations of old timepieces. They refurbish them, polish them up, change batteries and springs and whatnot, then we sell them. We even have one gentleman who'll put an inscription on one for you—if there's room."

"Wow," I say, looking back over the varied but uniformly shiny collection.

"You want to see one? You want me to open up the case?"

"I'd love one," I say. "But I don't think it'll be quite right. Maybe next time."

"Maybe," she says, and goes back to dusting. I think she really is dusting.

I find a blue stuffed cat. It is a lot bluer than Mrs. Kotsopolis's cat was, bluer than anybody's cat ever was. And I get a very small box of Belgian chocolates shaped like seashells.

I take the stairs up the three flights to where my mother said she is. I don't dare ask downstairs because if they didn't let my mom in to see her, I won't stand much of a chance. I will need to find her myself.

She'll have to see me. She will have to see my face, and then she cannot mistake what is inside me, who is inside me, and what I bring with me. She will see, and then she will let me sit with her, and then I will have the chance to tell her what kind of a man my father was and then we will see. That's all. Then we will see.

And we will live with what we see.

I pass a setup on the last landing before the top floor. It's a wall telling all about the hospital's radio station, which I have been hearing since I got here without even hearing it. I look up at the speaker above me, listen to some guy speak gently yet enthusiastically about Judy Garland, and then play "Over the Rainbow." The postings on the wall tell me that I, too could provide this service if I had some free time, a generous spirit, and an interest in music, conversation, and/or humanity. There is a request box which I look into and find a couple of gold Rolo wrappers and nothing else. Above the box, a stack of request forms is tacked firmly to the board.

I push my way through the doors on the top floor, and already I don't like what I smell. The whole building smells like a hospital, of course, but the farther you walk in from the street, and then the farther you walk up, from the street, the farther you get from the scent of air, and health, and happiness. This thing that lives up here on the top floor, far away from the entrance and the free world, is a thick and sad and chemical-covered blend of rot and poison no matter how wonderful the work of all the people trying their best here.

I chew gum. I chew half a pack of gum as I walk quietly along the walls like a rodent, trying not to be caught, trying to get where I need to get. There is a lot of busy here, and I try to just be one more part of the effort. I peek my head in the first door, and find one old guy, staring high up at a TV that isn't on. There is a curtain separating him and the next person, who barks for a nurse with enough bellow to convince me that this is not Helen Kotsopolis's room and I should get out of the way. Next room's empty. Next room is a guy sitting upright with his arm out sideways at a ninety-degree angle and a series of long naillike things sticking out of it. His hand doesn't look life color.

He reminds me of a story my dad brought home, of a motorcycle guy who took his bike out for an early spring slick-road test and by the time the Hothouse team scrambled, the bike was mangled and this guy and his shoulder were connected in just the tenuous way two sneakers are connected when they are thrown over a telephone wire. My dad and his pals got this guy and his arm saved.

I'm thinking this is that very guy. It doesn't have to make literal sense because it makes bigger sense than that. And the old guy staring up at the TV is the guy my dad pulled from under his car when the jack kicked over. And the kid right now, right this minute shouting for his morphine is the same kid who my dad pulled out of the river on Labor Day when he should have been fishing with me. Saved the kid so he could go on and do whatever other stupid thing he's done now to get himself hospital-ized. I always hated that kid.

This place is full of people owing their lives to my dad, is what I'm thinking. Including Mrs. Kotsopolis.

He was a great man. He was an extraordinary guy.

My time is running out and I start just looking for names on doors, and I am three doors from the nurses' station when I think I do read it, Mrs. Hel—

"Excuse me? Can I help you, sir?" a tall red-haired woman in a crisp uniform and a small smile wants to know.

"I was just looking for someone," I say.

"I figured as much, since most of our doctors don't go skulking up and down with a blue stuffed kitty under their arms. Why don't you tell me who you're looking for and I can help you."

"Oh," I say. "Ok, well, I'm looking for Mrs. Kotsopolis, Helen, Kotsopolis?"

"Right, and who are you?"

"I'm . . . a friend."

"Are you now? Well, sir, I'm sorry, but you are in fact here outside of regular visiting hours, in addition to the fact that Mrs. Kotsopolis is only a few days out of inten-sive care, so it's a very delicate time for her. . . ."

"I won't stay long," I say, "I swear. I just . . . want to have a few words, see that she's all right. . . ."

"Are you family?"

You would think that would be a simple question. You would think, if I were planning to be honest there would be one obvious answer and if I were planning to lie there would be another, equally obvious one.

I would say I am, yes, is the answer that feels honest right now, so I say it.

"I would say I am, yes."

"More importantly though, would *I* say you are?" the nurse asks. "Because, no offense, but you are not exactly conducting yourself in the manner of someone who is supposed to be here. Again, I mean no offense, but we are trained to take note of this kind of thing."

Trained pretty well, it occurs to me. I feel weirdly, distantly reassured by this, by the nurse's protecting the patient from the likes of me.

I don't feel like jousting with her, don't feel capable of it, anyway.

"Can't I go in? For even just a minute?"

She turns her head, craning toward Mrs. Kotsopolis's door, steps back, looks in the small dark window. I inch up and peek over her shoulder.

I see her. That is her, I recognize. I see her eyes, and I swear she is looking right at me.

"What are you doing?" the nurse says when she swings back around to catch me.

"Just . . . having a look in, like you were."

"Well, I'm *supposed* to have a look in. I work here. You don't work here, and you are not, I believe, a family member, so I think I'll have to ask you to leave and let Mrs. Kotsopolis get her rest."

"She's not all burnt up," I say, maybe too brightly.

"No," the nurse says, "it was more about the smoke than the fire . . . and who *are* you?"

"Does that mean you are thinking of letting me in?" I ask.

"That means I'm thinking of calling security," she answers.

Reflexively, I stick out both hands, offering the stuffed blue cat and the swirly shells of Belgian chocolate.

"I don't often get bribes," she says with a skeptical grin.

"Can you see she gets these?" I ask.

She takes them, holds them like you would if you were going to keep them. I know she isn't.

"Who're they from?"

"Russell," I say. "A friend of a friend."

A friend. Of a friend.

I was afraid to tell somebody I was my father's son.

I back away, and the nurse eyes me suspiciously. Suspicious, but not mean.

I head back down, down the corridor the way I came, and down the stairs. I stop when I hit the landing, the one with the setup for County Hospital Radio.

Requests, right. They take requests. They *welcome* requests.

I'm feeling pretty much like an insider at this point as I navigate the corridors of the place, my request form in my hand and my head down so as not to attract attention. Most people around here seem to have badges.

I knock gently at the door that says it's the radio station. There is a pause long enough to cause me to knock again, and a bit louder.

"What are you doing here?" asks the face that is just about visible in the doorway.

"I have a request."

"There are request boxes for that. Nobody comes here for that."

He's thin and middle-aged, looks slightly nervous, slightly irritated, like he would prefer to be alone with his music and quiet talk.

"You do interviews, though, right?"

"Technically, yes. We don't tend to get celebrities or news makers through here often. Or ever, really."

"Would you like to interview me, then?"

"Why would I want to do that?"

"I'm something like a news maker, you could say."

"What news did you make?"

"I didn't make any myself, actually. Yet, anyway; I suppose I might someday. It was my dad who made the news."

He sighs. I wouldn't say he was excited, quite, at the prospect before, but he is deflated now.

"Maybe you should send your dad down, then."

"Can't. He's dead."

That has a lot of power, when you say that to people. You can change tones and gears and temperature when you bring that into a conversation.

"I'm sorry. Jeez, I am sorry. Can I ask, is that how he made the news?"

I am anxious to tell this man that I am my father's son.

"Yes. But he made even more news after he died. You know about the fire? The one that took the two firefighters? And then the—"

"Holy smokes," he says, opening the door wider and pawing my shoulder, "get in here."

He calls himself Middleman Mike. Midday, midweek, man in the middle putting you together with great music.

There is a bank of long sliding knobs on a mixer, on a table. Middleman Mike slides one down and another one up and a red light goes on above his head as the music settles down.

"Folks, that was Shifty with a song that never fails to brighten things up, 'Starry-Eyed Surprise,' dedicated to Roy from Lesley. She says, 'Happy anniversary, love. We are going to get better and have many more starry-eyed surprises together.' Well, people, how lovely is that? Get better really soon, Lesley, from all of us here at County Hospital Radio."

He has a soft and understanding voice that seems to come from a body older and heavier than his own. He is good at this, I think, and I am glad I'm here.

"We have a special and unusual guest here, now folks. This is Russell, who has a dedication he wants to make, and a message to send. Russell is the son of one of the two firefighters we lost in the tragic fire awhile back. And there is a certain Mrs. K. currently staying with us to whom he'd like to pass on his thoughts. Mrs. K., if you're listening, here is Russell."

A second red light goes on as Middleman Mike

slides another knob, and the microphone in front of me comes live.

"Um," I say, surprised even though this is exactly what I asked for. "Hello. Well . . . I hope you are feeling well. . . ." I have never been as nervous as I suddenly feel right now. " . . . And all I wanted to say was . . . and I remember when you came to my school, still, and your cat . . . and I am sorry, Mrs. Kotsopolis, about your cat. He was a great cat. . . . My dad was a good man, Mrs. Kotsopolis, and a great firefighter. Things went wrong, but not before things went really, really, really right for a lot of people over a lot of years. He spent a great deal of time being truly heroic, before he wasn't. I am sorry, for what happened to you and your cat when he wasn't heroic. I'm sorry, and I know my dad is sorry. Very, very, very sorry . . . Mrs. Kotsopolis . . ."

When I stop talking—anyway I don't stop talking so much as stuff just stops coming out—the silence I hear is so huge here in the little studio and in the waves of the air of the rest of the world. Middleman Mike just stares at me for several seconds with I-don't-know-what on his face. Could be sympathy, could be pity, could be irritation, but I am without a clue.

"Dedication?" he eventually asks me, live on air.

"Right," I say, like waking up, "my dad had such a huge dedication, every day of his life, to helping—"

"Sorry, Russell, but I meant the song. You said you wanted to make a dedication to Mrs. K.?"

"Oh," I say, absolutely flushed with embarrassment and empty of ideas. "I, ah, I'm sorry, Mike. I don't . . . really know music. Don't . . . know what she likes . . ."

"Sinatra," Middleman Mike jumps in, "I am sure she likes Sinatra. So here you go, Mrs. K., from Russell to you, Frank Sinatra singing 'Moonlight in Vermont,' and after that we'll come back with the man himself to talk about how he's surviving the tragedy."

Mike does his soundboard thing and Sinatra starts his moonlight thing, and I begin a new case of nerves.

"I don't think I can do that, Mike," I say.

"What?"

"I don't think I can talk about that, I'm sorry."

"You say sorry quite a bit, huh?"

"Sorry."

"Listen, this is why you are in here. This is why I let you in. People don't just knock on the door and stroll in here just because they feel like it. People will want to hear your story."

Even that, just his mentioning of *people* who will be

listening and judging what I say, makes me sweat. "How many people?" I ask.

He shrugs. "Couple hundred, including staff?"

"That sounds like a lot of people."

"Well, if it makes you feel any better, at any given time probably a third of them are asleep."

"Well, that doesn't really—"

The phone on the wall at Middleman Mike's shoulder rings. It's muffled, like a regular phone being suffocated under a pillow but he jumps anyway. He stares at it for a second. "That only happens about once every two months," he says.

"Hello? Yes. Oh, hello. Oh, yes, yes, absolutely . . ."

He aims the phone at me. I take it, my head swimming now.

"Hello?"

"What happened to my cat?" Mrs. Kotsopolis asks. Her voice is not even a voice, it is so soft. It is more like just shaping words out of breath. "You know something about what happened to Omar?"

What have I done? Already, what have I done here? Nobody told her what happened, to blue Omar? For good reason, Russ, nobody told her what happened to blue Omar.

"I'm sorry, I don't know," I tell her. "I just meant that I was sorry about him getting lost. I haven't heard anything. I'm sorry."

There is what may be a long pause now. It could be other things. She could be catching her breath, or even still talking very weakly.

"Thank you for the gifts," she says. "I smiled."

I smile when she says she smiled. I smile broad and mad like an idiot, this is such uplifting news to me.

"I'm glad you liked them," I say.

Middleman Mike makes himself work busy, playing more music without talking at all, without acknowledging that I am even in his room anymore. It helps.

"I forgive him," she says, somehow even more softly.

I choke up at the words. I choke so much breathing is hard, never mind speaking. I pause even longer than she did. When I get it together, I say, "Can I come up and see you?"

She does not pause. "No."

"Oh . . . right. Of course. I understand. Well, I hope you are feeling better."

"Thank you, son."

One more pause. One more deep breath and a run. "He was a good man," I say. "My dad. And he tried. I know he tried."

I hear her struggle with the breath, pull in as deep as she can, then release it in shapes of words. "I know. I saw."

I open my mouth to tell her thanks, thanks, thanks, and how much better that . . .

But I get dial tone.

How can I say? How can I say just how much that means to me, what Mrs. Helen Kotsopolis said, all that she said. Forgiveness. Redemption.

She liked her presents.

I got more than I ever could have hoped for, coming here, more than I ever could have prayed for in making this journey to this hospital, and the gifts I brought were less than nothing compared to the infinity of gift I got in return from the wonderful Mrs. Kotsopolis.

She *knows* my dad was a good man. She *knows* he tried. Because she *saw.*

"You sure you won't talk?" Middleman Mike asks me.

Won't? We are well past *won't*. I can't even speak to tell him I can't speak. I smile and shake my head and I think he understands but there's no way of knowing for sure. He hands me back the blank dedication sheet I brought in, points to the phone number at the bottom, and tells me, "If you change your mind. At any time, if you change your mind. I know people would be anxious to hear everything. You do owe me, after all."

I take it and nod and feel like I do, in fact, owe him.

"Good luck, Russell," Middleman Mike says earnestly as I head out the door. Just outside, I find the nurse, the same nurse who was defending Helen Kotsopolis from me. I smile at her.

"How dare you," she says in a low and controlled and terrifying tone.

"What?" I ask, shaken. "What?"

"This explains why you were ashamed to say who you were."

"I was *never*—"

"He is *not* forgiven, and he never will be. And you are not forgiven, coming in here and manipulating a poor, fragile old woman who has been through far more than enough for anyone to ever . . . She may forgive you, but I can assure you that God does not and neither do most of the people of this town."

I don't do it on purpose, but I fall back, on what seems to be the only thing holding me upright. "I'm sorry—"

She slaps me right across the face, hard enough for the sound to carry clearly down the length of the corridor. She looks quickly off, since this is presumably not what nurses are allowed to do, but the radio station is tucked away. She is free, though, to address me as she sees fit.

She sees fit to slap me once more, though this time it is lighter, weaker, less sure but more sad.

"That is for you and your father. It is from all the people here who have to change dressings three times a day. Who have to pull away skin when they pull away bandages. Who have to look into eyes blinded white. Who have to listen to breathing so compromised it sounds like we've got snakes loose in the ward. Who have to teach people how to bend arms and legs all over again because they don't have the flexible skin that God gave them as infants. Who have to sit by the bed while patients weep for hours at their own reflection in a hand mirror after their hair and lashes have gone for good. So thanks for coming by, and making yourself feel better, but do us all a favor now and go home because it's not changing anything for anybody else."

She spins and pulls herself away with such force I am sure it is to stop herself from beating me senseless.

And at this moment, I wish she would.

I stand with my back to the door of the radio station, my face blistered in the heat of the rage I found just outside. The height of that fall is so great I'm still falling, and sick with it all.

HARD SKY

Monday night is Young Firefighters. Has been for a long time, which is why I am so well trained already, why I am ready to go already but I will keep training until I am beyond training and when they are ready for me I will be beyond ready for the job. Monday night is Young Firefighters, because it is.

If I was nervous that first time back after the long lay-off, after the events of the summer, then what to call this? The nerves slashing around my stomach are so wild and violent they are nearly audible. Maybe they are audible, but I cannot hear them and they will only be heard when I cross through this door and my comrades are there to make the sound real.

I make a low intense growl as I force myself to push open the door, the kind of noise warriors in movies make to buck themselves into battle.

But there is no sound. There is no sound, because there are no comrades.

I walk in, move farther in, to the middle of the very empty room. It's not quite gym size, but it is maybe ballroom size, and the emptiness is making it huge. There are piles of equipment, helmets and coats and breathing apparatus lined up on long tables along one wall. That's a drill, getting the gear on as quickly as possible. There are various climbing structures and obstacle-course items arranged all through the place. On the far wall, about twenty feet up, is a window frame. There's nothing but wall behind it, but it's a convincing-enough frame, stuck there to the wall. You have to ignore the ceiling that is only another four feet above the window. Hard Sky, is what we always call it in Young Firefighters.

There is a ladder at the base of the wall, and I go to the ladder. It's a tall two-piece reinforced aluminum job with a rope pulley to raise the second bit. It's heavier than the kind you'd have at home.

There is an exercise. To practice getting to that window to save upstairs lives. It's a two-person exercise.

But nobody's here. There's never been nobody here.

"Whatcha say, Monsignor?" I say to the slumping

figure of the victim. He's half curled over like a drunk in the gutter. I nudge him with my foot. "You want to help? Your chance to be a hero."

I am not surprised at Monsignor O'Saveme's failure to respond. I don't think I would have been surprised if he did respond either. I'm surprised lately at my ability to be surprised by things that shouldn't surprise me, and to be unsurprised by things that should.

I kick him really hard. His humanlike head feels like a semideflated soccer ball as it leaves my foot, smacks off the wall behind him, and smacks again, facedown to the floor.

"I'll do it myself, then," I say. I take the ladder from the floor. I hoist it, drop one end so the feet plant somewhat stably, and I quickly begin to wrestle the bulk of it toward Hard Sky before gravity and momentum catch on and it fights me back down.

It's a two-person job. It really is, but there are no two people here. I'm fighting it from the go.

It's not a long fight. As if there is a team of little gnomish but fat firemen climbing the ladder as I raise it, the whole thing leans against me, twists and fights and goes all awkward and right off my shoulder to the floor.

Crash almighty. The sound of heavy aluminum alloy,

clattering to the floor in a big empty ballroom of a hard sound-bouncing place is something beyond what ears and nerves should have to take. It's a smash-up that lasts maybe three seconds but appears to happen over and over in some kind of replay, or bounce, or echo or all of them, but it is hellish is what it is.

You know how sound can make you angry? How really bad cymbal sound in really bad conditions can penetrate your skull and drive you right out of it?

I begin kicking Monsignor O'Saveme. I kick him and I kick him. I kick him in the ribs and I kick him in the stomach and I kick him in the balls, and again, and I kick his head so hard and so many times and I chase him and do it more until the force of it and the swing-and-miss and weakness make me spin awkwardly, lose my footing and bang to the floor in a lump right along-side him.

I am face-to-face with where the monsignor's face would be if he had one.

"I'm sorry," I say, through really breathy, really halt-ing, hiccuppy panting.

"Have you got something to confess, my son?" The Girl's voice asks from across the room.

"No," I say, staying right where I am.

"Did you just beat up the monsignor?"

"Yes."

"Do you feel better?"

"I don't feel anything."

Like a sprite she appears in front of me, just beyond the monsignor. She crosses her legs at the ankles and smoothly allows herself to sink, to sit, cross-legged on the floor.

"Where is everybody?" she says in an incurious way.

Now I sit up. I cross my legs too. It doesn't work. I pull up my knees and rest my chin on them instead.

"Where is everybody?" I repeat back at her.

"I asked you that," she says.

"And I asked you that, Melanie. Just the truth, is all you have to give me. Just as long as you keep it true, we'll be all right. I'll be all right."

We have a stare-down. But it's not that, is it? It's not that, it's a stare-*up* because she is here to help me, to lift me up if lifting is possible or to catch me if it's not. She is, obviously. Look at her face.

"Melanie?"

"It's not on this week, Russell. That's all. They decided to give it a week. Two, maybe."

"Give it a week, for what?"

She shrugs. It is a shrug that does not mean *I don't know.*

"For me to go away? For me to come to my senses. Melanie, is that it? For me to realize it's not worth it and then just quietly melt away . . . hey, like my dad did. Did you get that? Melt away, just like my father did. That's pretty funny."

I've done it now, of course. I've brought the details back now, haven't I? I am seeing it, I am seeing my dad's big beautiful face, his majestic mustache, and I am seeing the flames coming up, teasing, teasing, licking, lapping, peeling it all back, from the lip on up and right back up over. . . .

"I'm here," Melanie says, leaning forward and insisting her face into my face. "I'm here, Russ. I hope that's something. Lots of people will be here, in time, if you just hold on. They'll be back."

"I won't be here," I say, and shock myself with the words, true as they feel.

"What?" she says, as if I had just declared my intention to commit hari-kari.

"I don't think I can do this now, Melanie. I don't know if I belong with these people anymore . . . or maybe if they don't belong with me. Everybody is so wrong. They're all wrong, I'm all wrong. . . ." I shake my head all around, like a wet dog, to get her face out of my face, to get the visions out of my head, to just shake, for godsake.

I grab the monsignor in a choke hold, and I begin pounding his head off the floor. I see my hands turning white with the effort, and for a moment I feel like I am accomplishing something right and important.

Melanie says nothing, does not intervene. Until I am exhausted, and Monsignor O'Saveme is seven times dead.

"I hope you feel better," she says, "but we both know you will be back. We both know it's not even a decision."

Her face is so close now, again, it is so there, I want to touch it. I do, very lightly, with two fingers of my right hand lightly brushing the sharp bone along her left eye. Then I go back to my hands holding my shins, and my knees supporting my chin.

"He was *Dad*," I just about whisper as she sits back on her side of the monsignor.

She just watches me.

"He was so . . . *else* from what you're hearing. I wish you could have met him."

"I almost feel like I have," she says. "DJ, that night, all night. That's all he did, was talk nonstop about your dads."

I'm staring now, and raise my head up. "That's all he did, all night?"

She smiles. "Pretty much."

That'll do for me.

"Would you like to?" I ask hopefully.

She draws back a bit. "Excuse me?"

"Meet him? My father?"

She puts her hand out to me. "It would be a privilege," she says as I extend my hand, we clasp, and pull each other up.

It's a beautiful location, on a rise amid the rolling hills, in the new part of the newer cemetery. You can see the Teahouse from where Dad lies. And you have a clear view of the part of the airfield where the small private planes take off and land.

I am leading Melanie by the hand and the evening is warm and clear, lapis star-fleck blue, the grass smells new-mint, and I can just this minute feel the feeling that life is supposed to be and that Melanie is promising it can be. After this, I think I will take her over to see that very Teahouse and tell her a story. And if I'm really feeling it, I will even show her a real death-defying climb.

Only we don't even make it as far as Dad. We stop about ten feet short when Melanie pulls me to a halt. I wasn't even looking, staring up and around, at the lights of the runways, the sky, the Teahouse.

It was a fairly simple headstone. Tallish, four feet off the ground, highly polished black granite. The usual name-date stuff. Tasteful.

Now it's all that, and more. A message, painted diagonally across in tasteful fire-engine red, says BYE-BYE.

"Come on," she says, tugging me gently away from the stone, down the hill, then not so gently.

"It could mean a lot of things, though, couldn't it," I say flatly, not even attempting to convince myself let alone Melanie.

"That's right," she says sweetly. "It could be read a number of ways. But right now, let's just not, huh? Bring me back another day. Walk me home now, okay?" She is tugging me down the hill.

But I am tugging her up the hill. And I am winning.

We are here now, back, the three of us.

"What do you think?" I ask her.

"I think . . . you folks have good taste."

That is no small thing. I remember thinking that, thinking about just that, when Ma asked me for my input. It was just the two of us, at the place that sells the stones. We considered everything, from all over the range, from like a pauper mini obelisk thing to a bigger-than-me angel who was actually managing to be in flight in spite of her weight. But I remember clearly thinking—possibly my only really truly clear thought from those days and nights—that people would look at this and comment on its tastefulness. I heard the words, in my head.

"Thanks," I say. "It could be a nice *bye-bye*, right? A warm sorry-to-see-ya-go kind of a so-long, couldn't it?"

"It absolutely could, Russell."

"Truth is important, though, Melanie. As long as it's the truth, right . . ."

"It absolutely could," she says firmly.

I stare at the stone for ages and ages. Silently Melanie holds my hand the entire time.

"Once they start taking it away from you," I say, "they don't stop until they leave nothing on the bones."

She walks around and stands in front of me, up close, between me and Dad.

"It's time to go home now. We'll come back again."

"Will we?" I ask, looking at her hard to see what I can see.

"We certainly will," she says, and blows a kiss Dad's way before pulling me back down the hill.

"He liked that," I tell her, and I'm happy for him.

* * *

This cannot go on. He is right there—*right there*. I go to my bedroom window and stare across to his bedroom window, and I know he is *right there*. This is insane. This is wrong.

"Did you hear?"

I am startled to hear my mother's voice behind me. She is standing in the open doorway, arms folded.

I sigh. I have not heard, but since everything that starts that way lately ends badly, I am not hopeful.

"She died," Ma says.

That's the entire conversation, but it is more than enough. She never had another home, after that one burnt up. Never had another cat. It was so many endings, that day.

My mother walks in from the doorway, sits on the edge of my bed, and sobs like a child, her head hung, her shoulders hunched and shaking. I walk in from the window, sit next to her with my arm around her, and join her.

Eventually, exhausted, my mother runs out of everything, tears, energy, consciousness. She tips over sideways, curls up, and falls asleep on my bed. I pull a blanket up over her.

I leave her there and head straight over to DJ's.

I am banging on the door, and nobody is answering.

The house is locked, DJ's window is closed, there is no sign of life, but *I* know that he is here. I just know it.

"DJ!" I'm shouting up at the house. "DJ, it's me. Let me in."

I hear not a thing. But I smell smoke. It's coming from the backyard.

"What are you *doing*?" I yell when I find him sitting cross-legged in the grass. He is staring, entranced by his work. His work is a very robust fire, burning on the patio just below the deck. The fire is his fort, the one his dad made him all those years ago. Then broke. Then made again. The old unmistakable odor of melting plastic army men is toxic thick in the air.

He is also stinking drunk, a half-empty bottle of vodka in his lap.

"I'm moving on, Russ. I am getting on with my life."

"Don't do that!" I say, running up to the fire but running right back again when the big heat blows me away.

"Poor old Helen, she just wasn't a survivor, was she? Not like us."

Not for the first time lately, I am blasted by very different, conflicting feelings as I stand between DJ and the fire. Uppermost at the moment is, I want to smack the hell out of him.

"Now is not the best time to be feeling sorry for yourself," I say.

"You're wrong. It's the best time. It's one of the few deep satisfactions in life, I have found, feeling sorry for yourself. And who's got a better claim now than *our*selves? Well, there was old Helen—and her cat—but now . . . ?"

I keep checking the fire. It's his fort. He can burn it if he wants to. And if it somehow makes him feel better, if we somehow do move on to a better something because of this, then I am actually all in favor.

But we know fire. And this fire looks a bit close to the house. I'm not moving yet. Not yet. I'm watching.

"Hey," DJ calls from his spot in the grass. I look over and he is offering me the vodka. I go to him and take the bottle, take a sip, stand over him as we watch the flames together.

"What are *you* doing here anyway, hero? Hero, junior? Must feel pretty good to be reinstated into heroland, huh? Land of the heroes? Bet you're happy with the way things turned out."

"What are you talking about, DJ? Is that what you saw? In the report? In the papers? That my dad wound up a hero and yours didn't?"

"Yeah, that's what I saw." He grabs the bottle roughly

out of my hand. "I saw that my dad was made into some kind of fiend, while yours got off as the courageous walking wounded, fighting the good fight against the odds. I think there was even a picture in the paper of your dad with a bloody bandage around his head and a fife and drum behind him. What did you see?"

"This is nuts, DJ, there is no difference—"

"No, it's all out now. They are implying that my dad was doing party drugs while your dad was taking hero drugs so he could work through the hero pain and keep up all the heroing. That's how it's playing."

"I didn't see that at all. All I saw . . . I saw . . . a community that needed heroes, was happy to build them up, and then got a shock when they were taken away again. They got angry. First they needed champions, then they needed blood."

"Well," he says, hushed, "they got that."

He leans over on his elbow in the grass, takes a swig, passes the bottle up to me again.

"Where's your mother, DJ? We have to put this out. This is dangerous. It's too big, and it's too close to the house. You know that. Is she in the house?"

"Coincidentally, my mother is at the Hothouse. With all the exciting new developments, she thought it was a good idea to go and have a chat with Jim Clerk and, I don't know, negotiate to get my father out of eternal damnation. I think she's wasting her time, myself."

"Come on," I say, "this is serious now. We have to try and put this out."

I throw the bottle on the ground and take steps toward the fire. Just like that, he is behind me, and pulling on my shirt.

"No," he says.

"Come on," I say. "You have done enough."

"No, actually, I haven't. My father's ashes are in there, and the fire needs to burn itself out."

He had just received the ashes this week. Almost redundant, really, so a third burning seems viciously unnecessary.

"Listen, man, I hear you, and I appreciate that. But you've done enough. You are drunk, okay? And this is too dangerous."

"More perfect, still. Drunk men and fire—my dad would be so proud."

I smack his hand away and head for the fire, but now it really is too late. Much as we know about fires, it is already beyond us even if I had DJ's cooperation, which I don't. The big fort, stuffed with kindling and tiny furniture, oily rags and newspapers—we are also naturally gifted fire starters—in addition to the brave little soldiers, has lit the pressure-treated wood of the decking, and the fire is climbing the deck as quickly as DJ and I did the day our dads finished building it together.

Seeing it is beyond me, he has sat back in the grass with his bottle. I have no choice. I very roughly drag DJ out of the yard. He lets me drag him like a dead body, and he makes himself weigh a million pounds. I haul him over to my house and call the fire department. I can barely get the words out over the phone.

"Yeah," DJ spits in the background, "let the bastards handle it. That's what they do, right?"

This is the second worst day of all time.

How could I not know? After all. I. How? Could I not know?

"Dad?"

He is supposed to be home now. That's why I woke up. Because that's what I do. I know, and I do, because we are tuned like that, me and my dad.

He is supposed to be home, and that is why I got up, and that is why I have been in the kitchen laying out all the tools and treats for one of our legendary two-man breakfasts.

In the middle of preparations I hear a car pulling up, a sound which at this early hour still, still gives my stomach a Christmas butterflies feeling, and I expect him and I continue going on about my business.

And then, he doesn't arrive. Ten minutes pass and he isn't in.

I go to the window, and I see his fat brown Buick there, hard against the curb. The door is open. He is not there.

When I get to the car, he is not in it. He is not around it or under it or anywhere to be seen. Back in the house I throw on some shoes and a jacket and I go walking.

I only need to go to the end of our street, to the playground where our basketball court is. I stand on my side of the street, look across the basketball court, across the Little League baseball diamond where I starred for his eyes, across to the kiddie playground where I can see him, my father looking from here as small as I did on that pitcher's mound way back when. He is sitting on a bench.

Since I see him, I feel less of the rush, less of the anxiety that pulled me here like a tether attached to my chest. I can even enjoy it a bit, watching him grow slowly larger as I approach, through the pleasing quiet of what is already promising to be a nice Saturday later, with the kids this place was built for swarming all over it. There is dew still on the grass, I can see it beginning to burn misty upward, and I have the feeling of walking through time itself.

He is asleep. I stop abruptly as I reach the climbing structure, the hand-over-hand bars by the rope ladder, the fire pole leading to the slide. I feel my fingertips searching my palms for the blisters and calluses I earned right here a long time ago. I stare at him for a few seconds before I walk up to the bench where the parents sat to watch their monkeys climb and fall and crash and lose and win.

"Dad?" I say, standing over him. He is slumped, that kind of asleep where if you didn't know better you'd think he lived right here in this spot. "Dad?"

His head lifts when I sit down next to him. Slowly he looks sideways to find me.

"Hello, boy," he says with a glazy, utterly warm smile shaped somehow like a W.

"What are you doing here, Dad?"

"Needed a little air. Just needed to get out, walk a little. I'm really tired, though. Really tired. I just came for a little air, 'cause I wasn't quite ready to come in, and I sat down. I just got so tired. I'm sorry. I just wound up here. I'm sorry. Breakfast, right?"

"Yes," I say, standing over him again. "Breakfast, right."

"I'm just . . . really tired, Russ."

"I know you are, Dad."

He looks very much like a man with no plan to move. Then he puts out his hand.

I reach out my hand and pull him up. I feel the weight of him, and the tiredness that transmits itself all the way up my arm. So I keep hold of his hand, tugging him along, through the playground, the baseball field, toward home.

"I'm sorry," he says, as we walk. "Sorry you have to do this."

I laugh, just a little. "Well, you did this for me enough times, didn't you?"

He squeezes my hand. When I was little, that was the sign that it was okay for us to cross the street.

"I did," he says, tired but bright. "I did, didn't I?"

"You surely did," I say, squeezing his hand.

How?

How did I not know? How? Did I not know?

He didn't fail me. He didn't fail me, or anybody else.

I'm so sorry, Dad.

I'm so sorry.

I'm so sorry.

I'm so sorry.

COURAGEOUS STAYS

The damage to the house was not tremendous, but enough to force DJ and his mother to vacate for a while.

Not so bad, though, since it means they are bunking with us for the duration.

Turns out it is kind of handy to have a connection to the fire department, when they have to make a judgment call on whether a blaze was arson or an unfortunate accident. Truth be told, I'd say it was a blend, an unfortunate arson, but sometimes truth be better not told.

They did a good job. I watched. We watched. They were all business when the job needed doing, the men of the Hothouse. But when it was under control, when there was no doubt, no danger left surrounding the fire at DJ's, I saw the way they looked at the place, the way they hung together and hung close. It was like a funeral, again. Again, again. But more, it was their way of love.

"It must have been, ah, surprising," my mother says to
DJ's mother, "to be at the fire station when they received
a call to your very house."

DJ's mom takes a long and casual sip at her tea.

"Quite," she says.

We are in the living room. This is where DJ will be
sleeping, because he didn't want to share a room with
me, which is fine. It makes sense. It's not just the huge
five-foot-by-five-foot memorial dominating one of my
walls, though that didn't help. We have ground to make
up and all, and really I feel a lot better just having him
this close again even if he had to practically burn his
house down to make it happen. So his mom has the
guest room and instead of sharing with me he is on the
couch here. Comfortable enough.

The phone rings and I hop up to get it. Not that there
will be any great race to get there first, as I am the only
person who answers at all these days. The frequency and
creativity of the hate calls we have been receiving suggest
a good few people have quit their jobs to devote themselves to the task. I had a ten-minute screech the other
day from "Mrs. Kotsopolis's cat," who has not got the
manners I would have expected. I have chosen to meet it
all, to listen, to not shy away, to exhaust and absorb their

powers for myself. It's working, as the hate rate has gone from two out of three calls to about one in three. And I feel increasingly unbeatable, like the mighty cockroach.

This one's not hate at all.

"Yo, Adrian," I say.

"Do you think if Stallone knew all the pain he has caused me over the years he might withdraw all the Rocky movies?"

Ma is staring at me. She has developed the heart-breaking habit of staring at me with complete fear and apprehension whenever I pick up the phone now. I'm trying to break her of it. I whip up my sleeve and flash my tattoo at her.

"God, put that *awful* thing away," she says, squeezing her eyes tight and holding out the stop hand as if the tattoo is going to come after her.

She hates tattoos. She hates the notion of my body compromised by any additions to what she gave me off the assembly line. But I know my ma, and she does not hate my tattoo.

"A party?" I ask in some disbelief.

"Yup," Adrian says confidently. "I just had a spontaneous great notion, and my parents have their flaws but they do know when they are powerless in the face of a spontaneous great notion."

I sigh. Sometimes his spontaneous great notions can really wear me down.

"What's the notion?"

"Bonfire on the beach. Right? Right? I figure, as long as you have a resource, a celebrity or something in your circle, you need to take advantage while you can before they get all famous and don't want to know you."

"You are drinking already, aren't you?"

"Yes. It's raining. Shush. So I was reading our little weekly local rag, and the story about DJ's wig-out was there, with a nice photo—"

"Idiots with camera phones . . ."

"God love 'em, where would society be without them? And I was thinking, DJ's performance art is just the kind of centerpiece that makes a party special. So, as his manager, I figure you bring him over, he MCs with his firebug thing, everybody goes wow, and we'll sell the embers on eBay for a cool million. We knew him when, right?"

I am shaking my head at the phone. This works for the room I am in, making everybody smile, and works for the guy on the line because he knows just what I'm doing.

"Don't shake your head," he says, "it's already in motion."

"To be honest, Adrian, who's going to come?"

"I invited everybody, just like usual."

Like usual. What's that?

"Again," I say, "to be honest—"

"Listen, my friend," Adrian says in a voice two octaves more serious, "how many people have you ever met who were invited to one of my beach parties and did not come?"

That, is an extraordinarily good point. But it's all new now.

"I don't know, Adrian," I say. "I am afraid nobody will come. Then, I'm afraid of maybe who will."

"Hey," DJ says to me, "ask him if there is going to be unlimited free beer like last time."

"Excuse me?" DJ's mother fairly shrieks. She needs the extra volume to be convincing, because her face betrays how much she would love this party to happen.

I relay both ways. "Adrian says the talent is always taken care of," I tell DJ.

DJ claps once and rubs his hands together like let's-get-to-work. "Right," he says, "as long as we're going to be pariahs anyway, we might as well be pariahs at the beach."

I pass along the good news, and hear Adrian get right up into the next gear. Just before hanging up I tell him quietly, "You're a good man."

"Do the words *no, shit,* and *Sherlock* mean anything to you, Russ?"

Nicest swearing to come out of that phone in a while.

It is raining as we make the walk to the beach.

"Of course it's raining," DJ says. "Anything else wouldn't be right."

We have Windbreakers on—yes, FD Windbreakers, we didn't even think about it, the only kind we have ever known—and they just about hold off the rain. The sea is just a little bit stormy, kind of churny. And like DJ said, appropriate.

"What are you expecting?" he asks as we bump along, heads down against the weather.

"My expectations are . . . modest," I say.

"A lot of beer for us."

"True. Upside."

We walk a bit more before he says, "I think you should do something about that tattoo."

The words instantly sting. We haven't really talked about it. I didn't expect it to stay that way.

"I have to keep it, DJ. I have to."

"I wasn't suggesting you wipe it off."

"Really?" This is good.

"No, just an alteration. I think, if you just take off the bottom bit, the *Courageous*, then it totally works for me."

First, I am jolted. Then I look over at him. He is all but bursting to laugh at his gag.

It is the world's most welcome, joyous vision right now.

"Put a lot of effort into that, did you?" I ask.

"No," he says, like he needs to. "But if you think about it . . . *Outrageous*. They were that, man."

A crack in DJ's shield. And the sunlight comes pouring in.

"They were that," I say, and we both get the notion to put an arm around the other's shoulder at the same time. "But *Courageous* stays."

We are walking up the beach this way as we close in on the house. There, arranged sitting along the wet seawall are the full array of party guests awaiting us. Adrian, Cameron, Jane, Lexa, Philby, Burgess, and a few people I don't even know. The people you would expect, if you had any expectations. I could scream with happiness at the dull wonderful reliability of them.

The music is louder than the last party, booming out over the beach.

Melanie is right there at the top of the stairs. And even a couple guys from Young Firefighters.

"Not bad," DJ says, gesturing for me to go first up the crunchy old stairs.

"It's a start," I say.

"Quality, not quantity."

Melanie gives me a kiss on the cheek, then hugs DJ. Cameron comes up, slaps my back and says, "Montgomerie says he'll be a little late. There was another party without an asshole."

That's the stuff.

"Are ya winnin'?"

My dad is not great at basketball, but he is effective. He plays rough-and-tumble, and every trip to the hoop by either one of us is a threat to my health.

We are at the playground just at the end of our street, the place that always inspires him to taunt and rile me up something fierce. I have just boldly driven the lane against him. He slid his bulky self over there, in my way, planted, and blocked me soundly. It was not exactly like hitting a wall, more like, if you've ever done it, running into a telephone pole that you never saw coming.

He is standing over me as I lie flat on my back

on the buckled, cracked asphalt. I can see out of the corner of my eye as the ball rolls farther and farther down the street.

"Can ya take it?" he says, smiling, provoking me.

The sun is behind him, peeking over his shoulder so I have to fight that, too. I squint to catch his expression.

"Course I can take it," I say, "I'm a firefighter."

"Ha," he says, satisfied. He sticks out his hand for me.

"Are ya winnin', son?"

I take his hand.

"I'm winnin', Dad. Hurtin', but winnin'."

"Ah," he says, yanking me to my feet, off my feet, "that'd be about right, then."